I0571541

THE CORNWALL NOVELLAS

DUDLEYTOWN

College sophomore Alexander Strauss has one rule: no messing around with straight guys. Especially not his mouthwatering roommate, Shannon. When their ride share drives off the side of a mountain, the two young men find themselves deep in an uninhabited forest searching for their missing friend. Wandering the famously cursed grounds of Dudleytown, Alex figures something truly unholy must be at play, because only insanity could tempt him to break his cardinal rule.

SIMPLE GIFTS

A former ward of the state, Jason Ferris is fiercely protective of his carefully guarded private life. When he's felled by a rogue lawn ornament at a Christmas party, Jason finds himself in the care of his first and most devastating love-- dark, dangerous, and equally damaged Lt. Robb Sharpe.

Newly returned from years away in the military, Robb's homecoming isn't exactly the stuff of fairytales. Now thrust together after a ten year hiatus, Jason and Robb discover that perhaps some things are worth waiting for.

THE CORNWALL NOVELLAS

Copyright (c) 2017 by L.B. Gregg, LLC

Cover Art by LC Chase

Book design by Kevin Burton Smith

All rights reserved

DUDLEYTOWN

Original publication 2010 by Musa Publishing; 2015 L.B. Gregg, LLC

SIMPLE GIFTS

Original publication 2011 by Musa Publishing; 2015 L.B. Gregg, LLC

No part of this book may be reproduced or transmitted in any form or by any means, electronic or mechanical, including photocopying, recording, or by any information storage and retrieval system, without written permission from L.B. Gregg, LLC.

ISBN: 978-0-9863132-3-3

Printed in the United States of America

This is a work of fiction. Any resemblance to persons living or dead is entirely coincidental.

THE
CORNWALL
NOVELLAS

DUDLEYTOWN

A CORNWALL NOVELLA
by L.B. GREGG

AUTHOR'S NOTE

Every day, I drive the twisted roads of Northwestern Connecticut. From high on Mohawk Mountain and down along the valley through Cornwall Bridge, I head to the higher elevations in Kent. New England's changing seasons unfold before me. The budding red-tipped forests in spring; the dappled sunlight reflecting on the Housatonic River in summer; the famously vibrant colors of autumn leaves; and the stark snow and bitter winds blowing in winter—the world in that thirty-minute drive, hundreds of days a year, becomes a feast for my eyes and a playground for my mind.

For a couple hundred years, the tiny area known as Dudleytown scraped a meager existence above Furnace Brook Road. My husband hiked the trails from Mohawk State Forest to Dudleytown and then over to Connecticut's sliver of the Appalachian Trail when those pathways were still accessible to the public, back when he was a teenager and the world was a far friendlier place. His description of the cool mountain roads which always lie in shadow and the empty spaces where houses once stood—as well as my morning commute and personal knowledge of this amazing landscape—inspired my short story *Dudleytown*. I hope that you enjoy it.

Halloween 2010
LB Gregg

CHAPTER ONE

The Jeep whipped along the twisted blacktop at a knuckle-whitening clip, and I knew—way before that cop showed, or we went airborne off Dark Entry Road, or any of the other creepy shit that went down in Dudleytown—that tonight I was going to get royally screwed.

"Flirtin' With Disaster" crackled through the broken speakers, the song weirdly prophetic, but Ricky didn't notice. He just hunched over the steering wheel and searched the desolate hillside for what he called his "secret shortcut."

A shortcut.

Right. He must be smoking something special tonight, because there wasn't a house or streetlight—even the stars were hiding. With the closed state park on one side of the road and the Housatonic River hugging the other, we had nowhere to go but forward on Route Seven. Every shop was closed, not that there were many lining this dead road. The one gas station was shut tight. Kent Falls loomed black as tar when we shot past doing fifty-five in a thirty. The only *cut* here was going to be the *extended cut*.

Ricky said, "It's somewhere on the right. Keep your eye out."

"I'm keeping my eye out. All I see is a lot of trees." Shannon's low voice rumbled from deep inside his sweatshirt. The sound made my mouth dry. He'd pulled his hood over his head and slouched against the passenger door, looking as energetic as an overgrown garden gnome. "You remember that I have no clue where we are, right O'Leary? I'm from Pennsylvania."

I piped in, "It's not like knowledge of the area helps." I'd lived two towns over from this stretch of road since fifth grade, and I still didn't know where Ricky thought we were going. Unless the Jeep could fly, the quickest way from Cornwall Bridge (where we were), to Goshen (where we were headed) was to stay the course. Point A to point B kind of thing. Only a moron would try to cut through the hills. Those roads were dead ends, driveways, or closed to the public. There weren't any shortcuts. Period.

"Keep looking, Alex. It's on the right."

I chugged my beer and squinted at the hillside. It was wicked dark out there. "I'm looking, but I'm not seeing anything."

Besides, I had my own shit to do. Like downing a third Bud Light and opening a fourth. Since we'd crossed the state line into Connecticut from New York half an hour ago, getting drunk and staying hammered until Monday became my new goal. I'd walked in on my roommate earlier today (the overgrown gnome in the front seat) getting sucked off by his curvy little study-buddy, and since then—man—I'd been pissed. The image of Shannon with his hazel eyes glazed, his jeans spread wide, and his cock at full mast had tattooed itself to the inside of my eyelids.

Shannon and I'd been roommates for two months, so I'd seen him naked before, but I'd never seen him like that. The two of them sprawled on top of my bed while she mouthed his huge dick, his big hand guiding the back of her skinny neck like a porn king. His nostrils flared, his perfect teeth sank into his bottom lip, and his chest heaved on every breath.

My own personal straight version of *College Dorm Suck-Off 2*—staring Shannon Murray—played right in front of me. Even so, those sweet hips lifting off my clean goddamn comforter sort of killed me.

I mean, why was he in *my* bed?

It had been weird and terrible and nauseating, and instead of kicking them out, or bolting like a good roomie should—silently shutting the door and retreating to the common room to tweet all our friends—I stood nailed in place, eyeing them like some kind of freak. Shannon having sex with his forgettable biology classmate had riveted me, and my dumb dick responded with a *schwing*.

Worse, what I wanted most in the entire world was to switch places with her. Dijon or Bijion or *whatever* was living out my deepest, darkest college roommate fantasy—*in my bed*. It should be *me* sucking Shannon. *Me* buried in that brown bush of hair. *Me* dragging those noises from his mouth.

At least, in my dreams.

When I finally managed to move my feet, I was so turned on I spent the rest of the afternoon hiding in the bathroom until it was time for us to leave.

Trapped in Ricky's shitty car, I wondered how the fuck I'd survive an entire weekend with Shannon. He lay flopped in the front seat, immobile and uncharacteristically lazy. His fists were buried in the pocket of his sweatshirt, and his head lolled against the headrest. He must be recuperating from his earlier exploits.

I finished my beer and chucked the can into the back of the Jeep. I wanted to whip it at my roomie's thick skull, but he'd have no clue why. I barely understood that urge myself, because, honest to God, I knew better. And even if I didn't have a firm rule about screwing around with straight guys ever again, he'd never look twice at a puny sophomore fag like me. No way.

A blast of light came from nowhere, and dazzling blue streaked the back window of the Jeep.

"Shit." Ricky smacked the steering wheel with his palm and hit the brakes in a belated effort to drive the posted speed limit. "Fucking cop."

I took a look, and blue light fried my retinas. "Where the hell did he come from?"

Shannon checked the rearview mirror. His rich voice shot all the way to my groin. "Hide the beer, Allie."

Allie. Worst. Nickname. Ever. When the geniuses at Residential Life first placed the two of us in the girls' dorm—*Welcome to Lakewood Dorm, Shannon and Allie!*—I thought the mix-up was another way to humiliate the gay kid. Once Shannon set them straight, they apologized with a free mini-fridge, and he'd saddled me with that stupid name.

I toed the six-pack under his seat with my sneaker. "Bend over and I'll hide it up your ass."

He snorted and snapped the music off as Ricky steered into a deserted picnic area. The headlights illuminated a stand of nude trees and silhouetted a crooked line of lonely picnic tables. The woods were eerily still. Milky fog climbed the banks of the Housatonic and crawled along the leaf-covered ground.

I threw my sweatshirt over the empties as the cop parked behind us.

Shannon finally yanked his hood down, and his tawny hair poked in clumps around his head. Older and wiser, he wasted no time bossing me around. "Just don't say anything."

"What am I going to say? I thought I'd just offer him a beer."

"And don't breathe on him."

"Shut it, both of you." Ricky wiped his forehead as the cop knocked on the glass. The window cranked, cold air blasted in, and the hair on my arm stood straight and tall. A beam of light swept the interior, stopping only when it pointed directly in my eyes. I squinted, trying like hell to look twenty-one, but I probably wouldn't achieve that feat until I turned thirty. I was a baby-faced towheaded boy. Slim, short, and perfect boy-band material. *Bye, bye, bye.* Since my hair hadn't been cut since July, I looked sixteen instead of twenty.

Almost twenty. Next week.

Ricky fished for his license and calmly handed it to the cop. "Is there a problem, Officer?"

"You got a busted taillight," the officer said around a toothpick. He leaned in, the better to see us, and rested a hand on the roof. He peered at Ricky's freckled face before shining his light on the ID. In the shadows, the cop's hooded eyes were bottomless pits. His gray hair was shorn military-style. *Trooper Phelps* his nametag read. He was thick as a tree stump, and his butch voice grated on my ears. "Goshen? You boys on your way there now?"

Ricky answered easily, "We're home for the long weekend from Tri State."

The cop didn't seem impressed, but neither were my parents when I failed to get into Cornell.

Lights flickered from behind us as a new set of blue lights whipped along the river road. This vehicle flew by without braking, and Trooper Phelps stood to watch it pass.

Ricky tried again. "I saw lights earlier. Is the road closed ahead?"

"Yup. You better find a different route. Cut back to Kent and head around Skiff Mountain, and fix that taillight before you take your vehicle back on the road. Not a good night to be in Cornwall."

The cop's light searched the car again, and this time, he nailed Shannon right in the eyes. My roommate didn't block the light with his hand or turn his head. As far as I could tell, he stared at the cop without flinching. His broad shoulders were stiff against the seat, and as usual, he didn't take shit from anyone. Not even a dude with the gun.

The toothpick twitched in the trooper's mouth. He snapped the Maglite off and returned Ricky's ID. "It's all over the news—big accident. Prison transport versus tractor-trailer. The roads ahead are blocked—you notice there ain't another car out here, right? It's eight miles to bypass the Cornwall Bridge and then you can backtrack. You boys keep to the main roads, you hear me? Stay out of trouble. And get that taillight fixed."

"Yes, sir. Main roads. Absolutely." Ricky answered, innocent as an altar boy. For once he didn't reek of weed. The cop must have bought it, because Trooper Phelps trudged back to his car. Ricky waited until the cruiser pulled onto the pavement and vanished. Within seconds, he spun the Jeep around, and we zipped onto the road, headed back to Kent. "We were *this close* to getting home on time." He checked the rearview mirror and made a sudden left—flinging me across the seat. "Shit, yeah! I'm ditching you bitches, because I have plans."

Apparently Ricky had found his shortcut.

A sign flickered in the headlight beams as we entered a puny back road. I wasn't surprised we missed this turn on our first pass because the freakin' road looked like someone's driveway. We climbed a sudden, steep incline, and the blacktop curved into a towering forest. I took a quick look behind us. "Did…did that sign say *Dark Entry Road*? What the hell kind of name is that?" It sounded pornographic—not that there's anything wrong with that—but still, it was weird. "Ricky. That cop said to stick to the main roads."

Shannon added mildly, "And here I thought the words *prison transport accident* sounded like key information."

Ricky grinned, "Oh, fuck him. We're only ten miles from town. I'm not driving all the way around the northwest corner just to avoid some on-the-lam jaywalker—this is Cornwall, not Brooklyn. And"—he drummed his hands on the steering wheel—"I've got a date. You ladies can play beer pong in Alex's basement and suck each other's dicks for all I care. I'm getting laid."

I'd like to get laid, too, but since that was unlikely, I kept my mouth shut.

Shannon mumbled something indiscernible. It sounded like *fuck you* although it could easily have been *good luck*. Whatever. I was distracted by the sound of rocks pinging in the wheel wells as the narrow strip of tarred road changed over to gravel. The Jeep's bald tires scrabbled for purchase, and even as we fishtailed, Ricky didn't miss a beat. "If the road is closed, you have options. You can turn back, take the detour, or, you can cheat. Think of this as taking the road less traveled."

Turn back, I wanted to say. "I'd take the detour."

"That's because you're a pussy." Ricky cranked that shitty southern rock again. "This is shorter. Chill. Have another beer." His grabbing hand appeared over the seat. "I'll have one too."

I didn't hand him a beer. "The sign said *dead end*. This is just like that movie—the werewolf one where the dudes aren't supposed to go out on the moors at night, and they do anyway. They wander around in the mist, and they don't live long enough to regret it because some fucking monster jumps over a stone wall and eats them."

"Well, no one wants to eat you, Alex." He laughed like he was a comedian, and Shannon punched his shoulder. *Hilarious.* "There's a dirt road that cuts through the state park. It's no big deal; I know these roads like the back of my hand."

"Yeah. We got that as soon as you couldn't find the road," Shannon said.

"I found it, didn't I?" Ricky nearly flung us into a ditch as the worming road cut sharply around the mountain and we skidded. "I love it up here. It's great for climbing."

"You mean it's a good place to get high."

"Oh, yeah. That too. Man, you are such a stick-in-the-mud, Strauss. I thought *gay* meant *happy*." Ricky's black Irish hair bobbled along as he drove without slowing over a log. "It's really cool up here. It's desolate and dark, and it stays, like, ten degrees colder than in town. All three mountains come together, so it's always shady."

Shannon peered through the window. "Shady is right."

"Check this shit out. They clear-cut the forest a hundred years ago, so now the woods are full of sinkholes. Pretty sweet for hiking, right? Especially when you fall up to your ass in a cave."

I pulled my sweatshirt back on as Ricky downshifted like he was driving a dump truck. The grade increased, and we climbed into the impenetrable darkness.

"This place has another name." He drove flat over the *No Trespassing* sign, still attached to its fallen chain.

"Are you kidding me?" Shannon peered into the rearview mirror like he expected the sign to get up and follow us.

Ricky ignored him. "This road goes through Dudleytown—it'll take us right through the heart of it and then down to the valley by Mohawk."

His words stopped me cold. *"Are you shitting me?"*

I'd known Ricky for a single year. He was two years ahead of me, he and Shannon both, and he was a geology major. I swear to God all those rocks he collected were from inside his head. Goddamn ride share. Shannon and I should have taken a bus.

"We're fine." Ricky insisted. "It'll take us ten minutes. Maybe fifteen."

"This ride keeps getting longer." Shannon's smoky gaze found me fuming in the backseat. "What's the deal with Dudleytown?"

Ricky cut me off before I could answer. "It's just an old ghost town. There's a story about the original settlers bringing a curse over on the Mayflower or something. They all went crazy and killed each other with axes. Some were hit by lightning or died under mysterious circumstances. You know, the kind of ghost stories we used to tell at Boy Scout camp, before we dared each other to come up here and spend the night. We used to scare the crap out of each other."

We did.

I added, "I spent the night up here when I was twelve." Which explains why I'm afraid of the dark and hate camping.

Ricky nodded, "Me too, man. Everyone says that the curse will make you do crazy shit, but it's just local folklore."

"You won't think it's folklore when they arrest you for trespassing."

"Arrest?" Shannon's voice sharpened. "That's not on my to-do list for this weekend, O'Leary. You better have this shortcut figured out, because I'm not risking my scholarship."

"Except when you buy your underage roommate beer, right? Don't get your panties in a wad. Alex is a pussy. And it's too late now, anyway. We're already in Dudley. It's just a bunch of old chimneys and foundations and footpaths. No big deal."

"Great." I wasn't happy. We were officially smack in the middle of flipping nowhere. Three miles in every direction to a house, a store, a phone.

The road took a sharp left toward another steep grade—this one with no guardrails. We winded down the mountain road as fast as a runaway train. I proved how much of a pussy I was by saying, "Slow down."

Ricky hit every stick and piece of fallen debris that littered the glorified hiking trail. In the circle of headlights, a deep ditch, chock-full of boulders, snaked blackly along the uphill edge of the road. A cliff marked the downside slope. That sheer drop of Connecticut ledge disappeared into the staggered tips of a dense pine forest. I grabbed the roll bar, and before I could say *fishtail* or *train wreck* or *slow the fuck down*, something large hit the hood of the Jeep with a colossal *whack*.

"Shit!"

The windshield smashed as a man's battered face cracked the glass. Blood exploded from his head like a splattered watermelon. Ricky screamed and slammed the brakes, but with no traction under the tires, we skidded on gravel and slid on pine needles. The man rolled across the hood, *thump-thump-thump*, and disappeared under the car. We ran right over him.

"Jesus Christ." Shannon's tight voice rose over Ricky's swearing. I clung mutely to my seat belt like a monkey, which proved to be a smart move, because Ricky cut that wheel, and we spun on the loose stone until the Jeep plummeted over the edge of the unguarded road.

We were airborne, sailing over the treetops straight from one horror scene and smack into another. We transitioned to the tune of jagged limbs clawing the windows.

Shannon screeched, "Hang on!"

Two tons of Jeep hit the trunk of a towering pine with a terrible *thwack*. There was a crunch of metal and the crash of broken glass, but my seat belt did its job as momentum flung me toward the back of Ricky's seat. The strap locked me in place and cut into my shoulder. My chin hit my chest with a bite, and Shannon's outstretched palm walloped me mid-chest.

We sat stunned stupid until Shannon hit the music, snapping it off with a click, and tossed his seat belt. "Everyone okay?" The sudden silence was almost as shocking as the accident. "Alex, man, you good?"

Ricky moaned wetly. "What happened?"

I couldn't get enough air to answer either of them. My armpits ran sticky with sweat, but I was chilled to the bone.

Holy shit. Holy shit. We hit someone.

A man had literally dropped from the sky and landed on us like a piece of overripe fruit. He'd disappeared under the grill, and…he was somewhere on the road above us.

"We were in an accident." Shannon's words were directed at Ricky, but he frowned back at me, waiting for an answer.

"I'm okay…I think so." I unbuckled and rolled my shoulder. "My chest hurts where you nailed me, but otherwise, I'm good. You okay?"

"Fine." Shannon used both boots to kick the door. It didn't budge, so he hauled himself through the open window. The Jeep hissed and ticked in protest. "Check O'Leary. I'm not good with that—"

"I got him." I crawled into the passenger seat, and one look at Ricky explained Shannon's pallor. "Hey. You all right?" I grabbed my backpack and dug for a clean T-shirt.

"Yeah. I...my head hurts." Ricky jerked to open the door, but his wrist was limp and bent sideways. He moaned. "I think I hit the steering wheel with my face."

I flipped the light. Ricky looked just like an extra from one of my ghoulish horror flicks.

His nose was smashed. Blood poured from his nostrils, and the gash over his eye opened to the bone. At least, I think it was bone. "You're bleeding. You cut the shit out of your face and your wrist is broken." Somehow I knew to speak bluntly. It was cold in the Jeep with the windshield gone, but Ricky's teeth frickin' chattered because he was going into shock.

I searched my mind for everything I'd learned about first aid from my parents, the Doctors Strauss. I knew embarrassingly little. Pre-med and all I could think was, *Wow. Someone should call an ambulance.*

"Press this against your eye with your good hand—hold it there. I won't be a douche and lecture you about seat belts."

"Thanks for that." He smiled, and a red river of blood flowed across his teeth.

Gross.

I pinched the bridge of his nose, and while Ricky hissed and swore, I called to Shannon. "We need an ambulance." That was all I had. I was only a sophomore.

"Well, we're not getting one out here on this *shortcut*. No cell service, no houses, no traffic, nothing. You need to deal with him. We have to walk two miles or so down to the road, or we're going to sit here and wait for the second coming." Shannon glared at the hood of the Jeep as if the force of his anger could free us from this mess. "We're lucky we're not dead."

Someone else is dead, though.

Ricky cursed from under my T-shirt bandage. "My fucking car. What did we hit? I swear some dude fell out of a tree—but it was a deer, right? Tell me it was a deer."

Shannon took charge. "Wait here. Is there a flashlight? Flares? Anything useful?"

"In the back. There's a tool box—flashlight and some ratchets and…I need to puke." Ricky gagged and opened his door.

Shannon swallowed, and I knew he was fighting his own nausea. He didn't glance our way when he barked, "Take care of him, Allie. I need to check the road."

"Just don't pass out." I spoke to them both. Shannon's aversion to blood was legendary, which left me to deal with the blood and vomit— the very hallmarks of my future career. I got busy as Shannon climbed to the road, his footfalls strangely muffled in the pine forest.

I dug through my bag for my first-aid kit. My mother packed it when I first left for college last year, but now the contents were meager: a half-empty box of Band-Aids, a tube of Neosporin, an empty bottle of aspirin, a pair of plastic tweezers, and a condom.

Wa-hoo. I was prepared to have safe sex and/or remove a splinter.

Ricky dragged his sleeve across his mouth and stared through the missing windshield. Crumbled safety glass littered the dash like scattered marbles. "My dad's gonna kill me."

"Don't think about that now. Keep pressure on your face. We need to get out of the car." The blend of gas fumes, blood, vomit, and beer was too much for me. I should be shaking with adrenaline, but I guess helping Ricky kept my head together. "Do you hurt anywhere else?"

"No. I…don't think so. My wrist hurts—and my face."

I shimmied through the window and dropped to the ground. It was much farther than I expected. My feet hit the pine needles, and I sucked in the clean fragrance of Christmas. When I exhaled, my breath made a cloud in the cold air. We were surrounded by a black emptiness. There were no stars, no houselights; even the moon hid its face. There was nothing here to offer a speck of light or a fleck of hope, just the headlights blaring furiously into the trees. I hovered close to the side of the Jeep, while Ricky vomited without restraint onto the forest floor.

We'd actually stopped *in* the pine tree, the Jeep cushioned by thick lower branches, and a blanket of forest growth lay tangled under the chassis. Beyond the glare of the headlights, it was bloody fucking dark on the edge of Dudleytown.

I hate the dark. I hate it enough that I still sleep with the light on—which by some miracle, Shannon had never mentioned.

The vision of Shannon and his co-ed sex partner had finally disappeared from my mind's eye. Unfortunately, it had been replaced by that man's ghastly face smashing the windshield. Blood smeared the ruined hood of the Jeep…and it had to be on the grill and coating the tires.

The pine scrub gently cradled the Jeep, and I couldn't force myself to look under there for anything. I just knew gore, carnage, guts, and worse slimed that undercarriage.

"We're good and stuck." Shannon materialized from the trees, and I jumped a foot in the air.

"Could you not do that?"

The Jeep lurched on its tree bed as Shannon joined me. "Get your shit together."

"I'm fine."

"No, I meant that literally. Get your crap from the Jeep."

"Oh." I kept my voice low. "I think Ricky has a concussion. Did you see anything?"

Like a dead guy lying in the road?

Spooked, I scrubbed at my hair, and only when my fingers stuck to the strands did I remember Ricky's blood covered my hands.

"Nothing. Whoever he is, he's gone. There's blood, but it just ends in the dirt." Shannon grabbed our stuff and shouldered his and Ricky's backpacks. He handed me my pack. "Put this on, Allie. Fix him up, and let's get the fuck out of here."

CHAPTER TWO

It took about five minutes to jury-rig a sling and tape Ricky's eyebrow together with Band-Aids. Nothing could be done about his nose, but the bleeding had stopped on its own. Now he resembled Frankenstein's wild stoner cousin. He was ill; he was swelling. And he kept muttering, "Fuck, my dad's going to kill me," like we hadn't heard him the first four hundred times.

Still. We were alive. I focused on the positive and got Ricky to his feet.

Shannon handed me a flashlight and dealt with the Jeep. He wisely packed the empty beer cans. "Let's go."

Ricky stumbled after me. "Did we—was there a guy? Did we hit someone? I can't remember."

Shannon and I exchanged a look before he cut the Jeep's lights. The darkness was complete. I could only hope that when we got to a clearing, there would be moonlight. I flexed my hands against the chilled air and latched on to Ricky's sleeve. "We're going to check and see. Let's get up the hill first. One problem at a time."

"But…my car."

"It's totaled, bro. We'll come back in the morning." My mother would have asked if Ricky had Triple A. They would have come in handy because that Jeep was shish-kabobbed until someone with a winch could haul it back to the road. "Keep moving. We need to stay together."

Nothing good ever happens to the one moron with the flashlight who gets separated from his friends and wanders lost in the woods. That's like scary movie one-oh-one, and I'd seen every Halloween movie in existence. I kept my hand on Ricky, who was panting his puke breath down my neck, and we followed on Shannon's heels.

The occasional screech of an owl, the noises of the night, bats swooping, the crunch of pine needles, and the snapping of twigs by unseen feet...this entire scenario spooked the piss out of me, but I climbed resolutely up the hill. It was less easy than it sounds. There wasn't a trail, only a ledge of slippery rock and scrubby pine and nothing to hang on to but sheer grit and determination. I kept my flashlight beam steady on the ground and crashed into Shannon's back more than once.

He tolerated me, but only just. "Watch your feet."

"I'm trying, but you need to move your ass out of my face." He kept stopping short. It's possible I followed too close.

Eventually, we arrived at the scene of our accident. I tried to look everywhere at once, but there wasn't any sign of the man who fell from the trees. No abandoned corpse lay battered in the dirt. The road was deserted, and the Jeep had torn it to shit.

Shannon didn't waste a moment in reflection. "I need you to wait here." He nodded toward Ricky who had collapsed with a groan and now cradled his wrist close. "Keep an eye on him."

"Wait?" An owl hooted, and I dropped the flashlight. "Are you fucking crazy? I'm not waiting here. Where are you going?"

"I'm going ten feet away. I need to double-check the road. I could have missed something. Just mellow out and wait for me."

"Fine." Too keyed up to sit in the gravel with Ricky, I let Shannon walk away—he didn't go far—and grabbed my light. I checked my cell phone again. No bars, no service, nothing. No power, either. I tucked that worthless piece of crap into my pack and searched the woods with the flashlight for signs of a gravely injured person or a dangerously loose convict. The cop had said "prison transport accident" and, with the roads closed below, I could only assume a felon would seek the high ground. Of course, we were on the highest ground. I stared into the ravine where we'd left the Jeep.

Maybe we should have stayed with the car.

Ricky's sick gasp broke through my thoughts. "It didn't seem like we'd gone that far."

"We were going pretty fast. When a car skids at forty miles an hour on loose rock, and you factor trajectory, as well as the pitch of the mountain into the equation—"

"Fuck you, Strauss, I know this was my fault. Just say it."

"Hey. Calm down, man. I didn't accuse you of anything, I was thinking out loud. Consider it a word problem. I like math." Such bullshit, because this was undeniably his fault. "You're the only one who knows where the hell we are, so which way should we go?" I shined my flashlight toward the ominous black void of Dudleytown. "That way?" A bad idea in my personal opinion. "Or back to Route Seven?"

I pointed the light uphill, and Shannon appeared in the yellow beam. He stared mutely at the treetops as his flashlight cast a diffuse circle into the pines. Behind him? The road was another ominous black void.

Ricky wheezed and swiped at his face with his shirtsleeve. "We're better off hiking through the state park on the trail. It's the shortest way back to Furnace Brook. It's right next to the road. The gas station has a phone. Or we could stay on this road. There's a line of houses at the bottom, I think. It's a couple miles or so that way." He pointed toward Dudleytown.

"That's...not too bad," I said evenly.

"We're out in the middle of fucking nowhere—go on say it. *This is my fault.*"

"Hey. Calm down, man. Let me see your eyes." He let me, but stared with such malevolence one would think I'd gotten us into this mess. His green eyes were bloodshot and wild, and one pupil remained dilated in the light.

Not a good sign by any measure.

"Allie." Shannon's light zeroed in on my face.

This wasn't the time, but I was getting sick of that name, not to mention his fucking light blinding me.

"Come look."

I handed Ricky my flashlight. "Sit tight. Don't move. And don't go to sleep."

"Why would I do that?"

"I don't know, but stranger things have happened."

I trudged up the sloping road, knowing that with each step, there could be blood under my shoes. Some crime scene investigator would have a field day with the mess we were making. I sweated the forty dark steps to Shannon, tripping over the rubble and rocks littering the ground. As long as I wasn't stepping on a dead body, or its dismembered parts, I guess that was all right. "Did you find him?"

With a glance at Ricky, Shannon kept his voice from carrying. "No."

He loomed in front of me. The two backpacks made him even bigger—like the Incredible Hulk. Taller, stronger, and more self-assured, he didn't look affected at all by the accident. If anything, he'd grown more alert and in control than ever—which must be his personal response to danger. Large and in charge while the rest of us cowered and puked.

"Take a look."

I followed him to the edge of the gulley. "Where the hell did that guy come from?"

"I think he fell from the ledge. He could have gone this way." A deer trail divided the scrub. "You think O'Leary can hold tight while I look?"

"I don't know." I glanced back at Ricky, who thoughtlessly snapped his light off. "We should bring him with us."

"Bring him? Are you nuts? Just stay here and I'll go look."

I swallowed. This was another "what not to do" movie moment. Hadn't Shannon ever seen a *Friday the 13th* movie? Not only was there no way I would wait alone in these woods with Ricky—if that made me a pussy, so be it—but I wasn't letting Shannon take off alone again. Anyone could be out there. *Watching us.* "We need to stick together. Remember what that cop said about the accident."

Shannon's flashlight moved from the treetops.

"Shit. I completely forgot about that." Shannon rubbed his palm over his forehead and squeezed his eyes shut. His light illuminated his hiking boots, and I didn't want to look too closely at what might be stuck to them. *"Jesus."* He said, "Could we have one disaster at a time?"

"No. You don't get to pick and choose. How could you forget a prison transport accident—"

"Maybe because we just ran someone over and nearly got pole-axed by a tree."

"Well. It gets worse because we've landed in Dudleytown."

"Allie. You said that about ten times. So fucking what? Maybe a car will drive by, and we can hitch a ride."

There we stood in the middle of a hiking trail turned country back road, which *literally* had grass sprouting from its center line, and he thought a car would happen to drive by?

"Did you hit your head, too? Listen to me. We are totally isolated. You're Mr. Outdoor Leadership. We're practically on the Appalachian Trail. Only freaks come to this place in October because they think they can resurrect the dead."

He gave me a flat look. "I know you. You're too smart to believe in that crap."

"I know *I* don't. But other people ignore practical history and they come here to perform séances and drop acid. Or they come here to scare the shit out of each other. They collect phantasmago-rical data on their *Ghostbusters* machines and shoot blurry videos for YouTube and—not kidding—they get arrested for trespassing and disturbing the peace. It's enforced." I looked around. "Though not tonight because all the troopers are searching the bottom of Coltsfoot Mountain for escaped convicts. Anyone we run into here? We don't want what they're selling."

I took a breath. Shannon quietly absorbed my monologue as the wind shook the pines. Needles landed on the ground like rain. Any second now, a coyote would howl, and I'd fling myself at my room-mate. Even if he looked irritated with me for pointing out the facts, he exuded safety. He was a rock. A rock I could hide behind.

He finally spoke. "We should go back the way we came. At least there are cops on that road. And it leads to town. What do you think?"

"Well, Ricky wants to bypass this road and take the shortcut on a hiking trail. It's the quickest way back to Route Seven."

"I'm not taking another one of his cheating shortcuts. I asked you what *you* think."

"We should backtrack on Dark Entry Road, felons or no, and flag down a cop."

It was the obvious choice. Go back.

"Right. Let's do it."

"Fine." Now that we had a consensus, we stood there like tools doing nothing. "We should look for the guy we hit, shouldn't we?"

My stomach turned, but I wanted to find him. Morally and legally, we were obligated, but we had our own injured party to deal with. Maybe the other man was fine. Maybe he had a hearty constitution and a resilient bone structure—maybe he'd eaten his Wheaties. Maybe he'd just gotten up and wandered away.

And maybe three beers was my limit.

Shannon nudged me. "He couldn't have gone far."

"Okay. Let's move. I don't want to stand here all night." We both took a step, but in opposite directions, and I snagged Shannon's sleeve. "Goddamnit."

"What now?"

"I can't fricking believe it. Son of a bitch. He's gone."

"That's why we're looking." Shannon's light flickered to the shrubs.

"No. *Ricky.*" I stared down the hill at the currently unoccupied road. "It's O'Leary. He disappeared."

CHAPTER THREE

We took off at a clip, the two of us armed with one flashlight, two dead cellphones, and three backpacks. I had my doctor-approved condom and Band-Aids, a bag of salt 'n' vinegar chips, and some clean underwear and socks. I also had a cracked iPad and my organic chemistry book. I was good to go.

Shannon carried my empty beer cans and his biology book and—I'd bet all my clean underwear—he also had a Swiss Army knife and a compass. I'm sure he had waterproof matches and a snakebite kit along with the flashlight he was currently toting. He might even have a superhero cape tucked in with his toothpaste and dental floss.

Ricky's pack was probably full of weed.

"He's looking for the trail down to Furnace Brook by himself." I could have killed him for leaving us, but he wasn't in his right mind on the best of days, and now? He must be stumbling around the state park like a zombie. "We should see his light—or hear him. He isn't exactly fleet of foot or light on his toes."

Shannon took the lead, his light straying too often into the swale. "He's got to be on the road. He can only use one hand."

I wasn't sure if it was my imagination or the history of creepies and crawlies in Dudleytown, or the thought of felons, dead people, curses, or the depth of darkness that encroached on us from every angle—maybe my eyes were just playing tricks on me, but I swear Shannon's light had faded. It looked yellower. Dimmer. Like it was going out.

A lone coyote yipped in the valley, and I swallowed my voice so I wouldn't embarrass myself by shrieking. I squeezed my fist so tight my fingers went numb.

Get a grip, Strauss.

Shannon grumbled, "Now what?"

I thought he was grousing at me, but the road branched and he stalled. I slammed into his back again. "Oof."

"Pay attention."

"Quit stopping right in front of me."

Shannon's weak light searched the ground. To the right, a path made entirely of grass and loose boulders vanished into the forest. To the left, the broken road continued through the mountains. He grunted and swung the flashlight in an arc. "How many roads are up here anyway?"

"I think this is it. Plus the hiking trails, but those have been closed for years."

Nailed crookedly to a tree was a No Trespassing sign, a Road Closed sign, and a threateningly informative notice that violators would be prosecuted to the full extent of the law.

Someone had spray-painted a penis on it.

"Seventy-five bucks for trespassing." Shannon spat on the ground. "He must have hit his head pretty hard to come this way because I don't have seventy-five bucks to chase him. I don't have ten bucks to chase him."

"Get over it. Do you see any cops? It's not like we're going to get a ticket for trespassing." No. We were going to jail for hit and run, driving under the influence, assault with a vehicular weapon, *and* trespassing.

Jail was not going to look good on my résumé.

Shannon raked his fingers through his hair again. "Where the hell did he go? How could he get this far ahead of us?"

"Maybe he's behind us." I cupped my mouth and hollered, *"Ricky!"* and, just as quickly, I regretted screaming into the bleak emptiness of the mountains. Something just felt wrong here. Something that kept the two of us quiet. My big voice carried on the wind, and the sound only made us more desperately alone.

A twig snapped, and I smacked Shannon in the shoulder. "Quit freaking me out."

"Quit being so jumpy." Shannon checked the ground like an Indian scout and pointed. "He went this way."

Naturally, Ricky had chosen the grassy trail that disappeared into a tunnel of trees and rocks. I expected to see a line of breadcrumbs, but all I got was a few chunks of deer shit and some footprints. "Great. Of course, how do you know that's from Ricky's sneakers and not someone else's?"

"I don't. Maybe it's one of those escaped convicts."

The flashlight winked out, and I choked. "Knock it off, Shannon. You're not funny."

"Are you kidding me?" He banged the flashlight against his hand. The light sputtered and then failed altogether. My hands went from adrenaline-numb to ice cold as Shannon fumed beside me. "Can you believe this shit?"

"Yes. I can believe anything right now. I can believe in the tooth fairy at this point. I even believe that you packed extra batteries." My voice cracked and night swallowed the air.

"These *are* my extra batteries."

My shoulder ached as if the temperature dropped another five degrees. I slid my backpack off, found my nuts, and glared at the spot where Shannon should be. I willed the flashlight to work. *Work. Work.* When will failed, I let my eyes adjust to the gloom. "You're always so prepared—"

His heavy hand landed on my sore shoulder.

"Ow."

"Shhh. Be still. Do you hear that?" Shannon yanked me against his chest. I was too surprised to do anything but dangle there until he led me into the thicket by the hand. He pulled me behind him close enough that my groin snuggled his ass with every step.

Except for the backpacks knocking me in the face and the blood on my hands...in any other circumstance, this would have been a dream come true.

Oh, fuck it. This *was* a dream come true. We were reenacting a moment straight from one of my favorite porno flicks: *Boys & Bears*.

Yes. This was absolutely *the* worst time to think about sex, but his calloused fingers gripped my wrist, and he dragged me into the underbrush and holy shit, his firm ass wiggled against my firming crotch. I got hard—I wasn't proud of it. My dick stiffened like a good not-so-little soldier as his hips kissed my groin, and once we stopped, his lips brushed my ear. "Shhh."

Torture. Absolute fucking torture.

I closed my eyes and stifled a moan. In that movie, the big guy, Duke, had fucked his little camping buddy against a sturdy tree trunk while owls hooted and coyotes howled in the distance. Naturally, they'd remembered to bring lube and condoms, and through good lighting and amazing balance they'd shucked their clothes (except somehow they'd left their boots on) and screwed as furiously as animals against the rough bark of a towering oak. Or maple. And no one had gotten a splinter in the ass.

Even so, I had *tweezers*…

But that wasn't on the program for this evening—so I got a grip.

We had a minor skirmish over who was shielding who. We could have alerted the mayor two towns north of there with the ruckus we made getting ourselves hidden behind our own sturdy tree trunk, until Shannon finally wriggled behind me, and his crotch ground into my ass. He clapped on to my biceps with his strong hands. "Stay put, Allie."

How could he be oblivious to the sexual nature of our position? I mean, really? He was on top of me, holding me, and speaking in that rumbly voice. The way he said my name…*Allie*…it was like sex talk. It was all I could do not to slide my hands around his hips and drag him against me.

Our bags lay in the dirt, and I focused on staying alert and useful instead of being mind-blowingly turned on. The minutes slogged by, but the night sounds were a great distraction. Chirps, ticks, snaps, and crackles. Wild animals. Wings. The wind blew endlessly through the treetops, and pinecones landed in the dirt like shrapnel. Shannon's breath waxed and waned, fluttering into my hair. My heart beat… heartily…and his chest pressed the full length of my back.

Frankly, he was a little closer than he needed to be.

There was movement to our left—down along the Furnace Brook trail. Someone was climbing the hill. I could feel a presence way before the sound of moving feet reached my ears. Shannon whispered into my neck, and his lips touched my skin. "Don't move."

As if I would ever.

Seconds later a man rounded the bend and loped along the path. Shannon's palm moved to the center of my chest, making this the second time tonight he tried to protect me. He hugged me into his body, and with a shake of his head, my heart leaped and pumped every last drop of blood straight to my crotch.

I held my breath, and Shannon held his too. His big hand didn't move as he wrapped himself around me, and the smell of beer and pine flooded my nose.

Danger passed in a blur of feet and broad shoulders. A man raced the length of the unlit trail without a stumble or catch. He paused at the fork to take his bearings.

At least that's how it appeared from here. I was certain of one thing—it wasn't Ricky. Ricky had an Irish 'fro—thick, black, white-boy curls. Ricky stood taller than me, but he wasn't as large as either Shannon or this mysterious figure. Ricky was slim and slumpy—a nutty geologist. This was a grown man standing at the crossroad, determining his path.

Shannon's fingers dug into me. *Still. Be still.* I could almost hear his thoughts. *Don't fuck this up, Allie.*

The figure moved; his footsteps crunched through gravel before he vanished into the bleak shadows of Dudleytown Road.

Minutes ticked by, and neither of us moved. Clearly, I inspired as much carnal interest in Shannon as a wet dishtowel, but I wished to hell I could say the same for myself. The scent of his skin flustered me. The feel of his hair flustered me. His hand on my chest...it fucking flustered me.

And the more flustered I felt, the angrier I became. "Would you mind letting go of me?"

"No. You'll bolt. Just be still while we think."

"Are you mental? Fuck you. Get off me." I twisted from his grip before he could notice my boner, grabbed my bag, and slung it on. "Neither of us thinks Ricky's down this hill. If he was, that guy would have seen him, so let's move. He didn't backtrack, that's not how he operates. He must have thought he could cheat through Dudley and make it back home the easy way."

"Okay. So we follow him." Shannon nodded, shouldered the bags, and said for the second time, "Let's get O'Leary and get the fuck out of here."

CHAPTER FOUR

We hadn't gone far when the wealth of pine needles covering the ground became a squishy carpet of decomposing leaves. Our steps were muffled, but the forest itself wasn't silent like Dark Entry Road. The hills were alive with the hoots and hollers of nocturnal woodland creatures. I didn't know what animals lived there, but I could feel their beady eyes marking us.

The moon finally arrived. With just a peek or two, it offered the sheerest shimmer of light. Dudleytown surprised me by being breathtaking in its own way, and not just because every pop and snap from the mountains had me catching my breath until—seriously—I thought I'd hyperventilate. What remained of the abandoned settlement was eerily lit by silver moonlight. White mist slithered along the ground. Sunken foundations hollowed this small section of landscape, and each empty space where a house once stood was now blanketed in leaves and moss and clumps of dried lily stems; some spots sprouted young trees. Disheveled brick chimneys protruded from the ground like castle turrets, and moonbeams sifted through naked tree limbs as clouds raced across the sky.

It was oddly beautiful, if a little lonely, and any moment, I expected a werewolf to come loping over the hillside to devour us with his sharp, pointy teeth.

Don't go out on the moors at night.

Possibly that last bit was from my imagination, which was admittedly getting carried away—but the whole scene was so *American Werewolf in London* I wanted to cross myself.

A twig snapped, and I bolted to catch up to Shannon whose long legs moved across the uneven road with conviction and direction. He plowed through Dudleytown two steps ahead of me and didn't give the place a second glance. We were outdoors and he was leading—clearly his educational path was well chosen.

I wasn't so sure about mine. I shouldn't have left my first "patient" unattended with a head injury. There wasn't a hint of Ricky O'Leary having come this way. He'd utterly vanished. He could have plunged headlong off a cliff, and we wouldn't know until daybreak. He could be lying broken in a ditch, jackals circling his corpse and buzzards pecking at his eyes—

Really? It would be best to concentrate on finding a house with a phone.

I tripped over another rock. "You think we should use Ricky's lighter?" As if that could light our way? Still, a spark in the dark wasn't such a bad idea—and the phones were dead.

"What are you talking about?" Shannon stopped cold.

I smacked the back of his head. "If you stop short one more time, I'm going to hamstring you."

Shannon snorted with amusement. "You could try."

"Ricky has a lighter. It's for his bong or whatever he smokes his stash with."

"Are you kidding me?"

"No. The moon's out now, but once we get through here it's going to be pitch dark."

Unforgivably dark. We were likely to fall off a ledge ourselves. Like lemmings.

Shannon dropped Ricky's bag, and it landed in the dirt with a thud. He unzipped it and commenced excavating. "What the hell? O'Leary has a load of rocks in here. No wonder this thing is so heavy."

"He's a geology major. He likes rocks." That gave me pause. Ricky knew the area pretty well, having hiked here often enough, so maybe he knew some secret rock collector's shortcut. Furnace Brook was famously full of slag and deposits of iron and copper, and maybe right this second he was wandering the town road, safe and sound.

Of course, given his current state, he could have totally spaced on Shannon and me. He'd forgotten the accident within moments of it happening. He could have amnesia. He was at one moment pissed, the next weepy. He could be wandering blood-soaked and battered and not have any clue how he'd gotten that way. It wasn't impossible.

Something jangled. Keys. A tiny light flared. "He's got a LED. I think there's some matches, but that's useful only if we need a fire." The LED flashed blue in the night. Shannon pointed the beam at his hiking boot, and it barely reached the ground. "It's only useful if you're unlocking something—it's got no punch."

Shannon returned the keys with their punchless light and slid his hands all over the bag as if he were feeling up that girl from earlier today. Bunion, or whatever her name was.

Jealousy pried my mouth open. "You know, you could have warned me."

"About the matches?" He unzipped the front pocket and plastic crinkled. "He's got a lot of snacks in here, too." There was another crinkle as he stuffed food back into the pack. "Twinkies." He waggled the pouch at me. "I have a thing for Twinkies."

"Seriously? You're not funny. Ricky always has junk food. He gets the munchies—haven't you ever smoked pot?"

"No. You know I'm not into that. It's pointless—and you can't get it up when you're stoned."

Hand to God, if that's true—*I will never smoke weed again.*

"I'm not into it either but...I mean that's what people do in college. They try new things. They experiment."

Shannon stared at me for the briefest moment as if what I said gave him pause. When he spoke, his words were clipped with care. "In this case, not me. And not you either."

"Who are you, my mother? I tried it. I didn't die."

"Don't do it again. No drugs in our dorm room."

"Man. What is your problem? I'm not going to bring anything into our room—I mean other than beer. Or, you know, the Jager. But if we're making blanket demands about behavior, you could show some common courtesy and hang a sock on the door when you're banging a chick in my bed." I sucked in a breath. I might be a little high-strung, but it was the principle of the thing. "A sock on the door is code for *I'm fucking someone. Don't come in.*"

"Shit." Shannon stopped digging through the bag. He sat back on his heels, his attention on me. His jaw clicked. Even in the gloom, I could tell he was appalled. He ran a hand through his hair and scrubbed at his face. "Oh, *man.* Did you see her?"

"Her? You. It was hard not to." Really, really thick and hard. "Yeah. I saw you both." Leaves blew around my feet as I waited for him to say something. The silence stretched. I couldn't tell what he was thinking, which was for the best, but I was thinking, *Drop this, Alex.*

An owl hooted from behind us, and I'd grown so accustomed to the night noises, I didn't even flinch.

Shannon said tightly, "Well, that's...*fucking* embarrassing. Jesus. Why didn't you say something?"

"What could I say?"

"I didn't think you'd walk in."

"Obviously."

Something crackled as he crammed everything into Ricky's backpack. "I didn't expect—I wasn't really...with it."

"With what? She sucked your dick. What's there to be with? Next time stick a Post-it on the door." I blinked, and there he was right behind my eyelids again—his dick big and slick; her head moving.

Shannon cleared his throat. "We've been roommates for two months, and I haven't—I won't bang anyone in the room. It was just... fuck. Allie. Look, she said it was an experiment."

"Experiment?" I think I spat that word. "Well, congratulations, Professor Murray. I hope it was a success."

Shut up, Alex. I wasn't some spurned lover. I was a stupid sophomore kid rooming with possibly the hottest senior in the history of Tri State College.

"That's not what I meant. I meant that head is head; you can't not get into it once someone is down there. I mean, whoever it is, it's...you know, hard not to react."

When had Shannon turned into a jerk? He was doing that guy talk thing that I found really offensive.

Unless I was doing it.

I said acidly, "I wouldn't know. I only have sex with people I like."

Total lie, but I wasn't going to discuss my former whorish high school ways with Shannon while we bickered on that cursed ground. I'd had sex with plenty of guys I didn't like—and I always regretted it. Always. Because, too late, I learned that those dudes thought it was a good time to knock me around *after* I jacked them off.

They don't call it bad judgment for nothing.

Shannon hoisted the bag of rocks onto his shoulder. "I do too."

I should end this. We should be looking for Ricky, but I blathered, "Next time, stay the fuck out of my bed. I don't need your stuff on my sheets."

Lies. Oh my God, I wanted his *stuff* all over my sheets. I wanted his *stuff* all over me.

Shannon's eyes bore into me. "I didn't want that to happen, with her, and even if I did, that didn't mean anything. But I…" He floundered, and I thought he was finished. "I was more comfortable in your bed."

I could hear how red-faced he was, but screw him. "Who are you? Goldilocks? This bed is just right? Keep your dick and your chicks out of my bed."

"I already said it wouldn't happen again," he snapped.

What the hell did I expect him to say? *I'm sorry I had sex with someone other than you in your bed while you watched, Allie?*

Obviously I did.

He grabbed my arm. "Hey. Look. Are you mad? I'm…I'm sorry, Alex."

Okay, apparently an apology *wasn't* enough for me. "No. I am *not* mad," I lied and shook him off. "You don't answer to me. You do whoever you want. I don't care." Man, I could just lie all night long. "Let's move. We need to get down to the valley and find Ricky."

He glared for a fraction longer. "All right. Fine. How much farther?"

"You keep asking me this as if I know the precise distance. *I don't know.*"

A scream punctuated my childish outburst like a sinister exclamation point. A single voice echoed from the black nothing of Dark Entry Road, now a good half mile behind us. It wasn't a coyote or a bobcat. It was the terrible sound of an animal suffering the cruel hand of fate. The scream resonated through the chasm where these mountains converged, the sound unholy. As if someone's skin was being slowly stripped from their bones—a scene straight from another movie I'd recently watched, *The Hills Have Claws*. My hackles rose, and I gripped Shannon's shoulder and shoved him behind me. He seemed more stunned than I was, but I needed to protect him.

I swear to God: that scream belonged to Ricky.

Maybe. It could have easily been the guy we ran over earlier.

Whoever he was, his anguished call pitched higher until, with excruciating finality, as if someone had taken scissors, the scream snipped off.

Snip.

We were left to the somber blowing of wind in the treetops.

Shannon took a breath, about to say something, give some kind of direction or suggestion—*lead*, that fucker—and right down the road from where we stood rooted to the spot, a car started. I gaped. "Who the fuck is that?"

Headlights flashed. Someone was a quart low on steering fluid, because when those lights cut onto the road, the car protested in a frequency that made my ears ache. Shannon stood square in the center of the road. "That's…not okay."

"Maybe it's the police. I mean, they are looking for people on Route Seven." Which was on the opposite side of the mountains. "Maybe he was sitting in his car…waiting…like…a speed trap."

"I don't have a good feeling about this."

Cold fear slithered down my spinal cord because Shannon never lacked confidence. My limbs turned to ice. My breath puffed white in front of me.

Tires squealed as the car moved, and Shannon came to life. His hand slapped my shoulder blades, and he shoved me into the trees. *"Run, Allie."*

I didn't need to be told twice. I ran.

Sneakers sliding on wet leaves and spongy moss, I leaped over stones. I tripped on a fallen branch, and I swear a vine reached and snagged my ankle. The harder I tried, the more shit knotted under my feet. I pedaled fast, scrabbling with both hands when I slipped, until we came to a tiny section of clear meadow where moonlight flickered through the clouds. At a full sprint I fell like a stone directly into a fog-enshrouded hole.

Shannon landed on my back with a bone-jarring thud and knocked the breath from me. His jaw connected with my head, and Ricky's knapsack of motherfucking rocks rattled. I was pinned like an insect. Before I could suck a lungful of air in, his lips brushed my ear. "Shhhh."

Light flared. Even so, I couldn't see a goddamn thing other than a weird chiaroscuro of white headlight and black earth. We were both flat on *my* stomach in a gaping grave.

I was lying in a fresh grave.

Oh, shit. Someone had dug this hole for us, I knew it. We were going to be buried alive.

Please, please let this be my overactive imagination running wild again.

I lurched, scrambling to flee fast and far, but Shannon grabbed my hip. "Hold still. It's too shallow for me to move. We're in a sinkhole of some kind—remember? Ricky told us this. It's okay. Just be still."

His weight held me—and his words calmed me. I nodded into the dirt and tried like hell to keep my shit together. I panted into the freezing loam and robbed heat from Shannon, who radiated virility and clearheadedness. His presence eased my lingering anger and soothed my irrational fear of the dark—and my certainty that we were moments from reenacting another B-grade classic—*Buried Alive*.

At least we hadn't landed on a corpse or in a vacant coffin, right? Just a filthy trench of some sort that was in no way, shape, or form an actual grave. No zombies here. No vampires or claw-toed were-wolves...this wasn't a cemetery.

It was just a haunted ghost town.

No worries.

I spat leaves, and Shannon held me closer. "Quiet."

"Why?" I whispered. "It's a car. It's not like they can hear us."

"I don't know. I feel like it's imperative that we should be quiet. So shut up." That was reason enough. He had superior hearing and amazing athletic prowess. He was the bruising outdoorsman; I was skinny and small and here in case of an emergency, so I did as he said.

Shannon's breath huffed softly against my skin. His eyes in shadow, he searched my face. His stare strayed to my mouth. "You good?"

The temperature inside our cramped space went from freezing to sizzling. He shifted a millimeter forward, his hips rolled into my ass, and a charge of electricity snapped between us like a match lighting tinder. Fire whooshed through my limbs.

I'd pined for him for weeks, and the reality of Shannon…*mounting* me, because there was no other word for our position, well, it might finally be too much. He settled between my spread thighs, and this wasn't my imagination—this was erotic.

No. This was fucking hot.

With every shift—his hips, his thighs, his breath—he teased me until my skin crawled with heat. His hands slid along my sleeves, and he gripped my wrists with his fists. I hardened so fast I had to wriggle to reposition my dick.

This time when he said, "Hold still—" his lips intentionally brushed my neck and I froze. I guess he did too. Some magical force must be at play because Shannon capitulated with a groan and buried his nose in my hair like he couldn't stop himself from inhaling me. His fingers dug into my skin, and he pinned me to the cold ground. "Fuck. I'm sorry. I didn't mean to do that. I can't help myself when you're…and I'm sorry about earlier."

Sorry? I didn't want an apology. Not for this. I swear to whatever God was on hand—Shannon's cock was every inch as interested as mine was. He jacked into my ass with that two-by-four he kept hidden inside his jeans, and whatever excuse he might give later, this was real. I wasn't misreading a mistaken touch or an accidental brush of his hand—Shannon wanted it. He wanted *me*.

Shannon breathed against my hair and delved deeper into the V of my legs. His thighs tensed; his erection pulsed. We squirmed in the leaves and dirt, the sound drowned by the chug of that unhealthy engine, and, *screw everything*. Call this an experiment if you need to, call it stupidity on my part because it fucking was, but I pressed enthusiastically back. I arched against him like a total whore and moaned into the earth.

Shannon Murray—my handsome, heroic, goody-two-shoes roomie—laced his warm fingers with my cool ones, and I couldn't scoot away. He manhandled me with his thighs and his hips, and I knew better than to let him. I shouldn't let him. Straight guys like him were nothing but trouble. I mean, *oh my fucking God*, he'd had a girl only hours earlier, *in my bed*, but somehow that fact turned me on more. Somehow having him here, right now, became visceral. *I needed him*. It was my turn to have him. I wanted him.

I'd wanted him forever.

Maybe craziness was Dudleytown's legacy after all, because dark need drove me to insanity.

Shannon crawled over me, and his teeth nipped together on the tender flesh of my earlobe. *Jesus*. He bit me, and I hissed and clawed the mulch.

"You want it, don't you, Allie?"

What did he think? I was splayed underneath him. Ass up. Leaves scratched my skin, and as I nodded, *yes, I want it*, Shannon's palm slid under my ribs, fast but determined. I knew exactly where he was headed. Inexplicably, my roommate lost control and—I shit you not—he crammed his cock into me like he wanted to yank my pants down and plow me. He grunted and panted. His palm wriggled under my shirt, his hot hand scraped my stomach, and those fingertips slid inside my pants. He was going to jerk me off. Right there in a hole in the ground. Fuck. *Yeah*.

I lifted enough for him to slither past my belt as he mouthed my neck. Wet. Moist. His lips closed, and he suckled the sweet skin below my ear. His fingers brushed the wet tip of my dick, and I nearly cried with hunger.

"Shannon—"

From the road, the engine cut, and the car sputtered a few times before dying completely.

Bang.

That was the end of sex time with my hunky roommate as the promise of Shannon grinding me into a blessed orgasm turned instantly to terror.

Evil lurked.

Shannon released me. *"Shhh."*

Lust evaporated in the cool, still quiet, and his dead weight registered. He was really fucking heavy. Crushed under Shannon, his backpack of empties, and apparently a sack of geologically significant rocks, I wanted to run headlong into the mountains and hide. I struggled to get free, and something in my bag exploded with a pop.

We both jumped like a gun had shot, but the noise was just my emergency bag of salt 'n' vinegar chips bursting inside my backpack. Any other time, I'd have found it amusing that my chips exploded before I did.

The headlights winked out. In the absolute darkness, the unmistakable sound of a rusty hinge squeaking carried on the wind. Shannon gripped my shoulder. He held two fingers in front of my eyes and whispered into my hair, "There's two. Be still."

"Get the fuck up." A voice…whose voice was that? Raspy and low, he sounded like a lifelong smoker—someone whose future included O2 tanks and biopsy and hacking loogies into a hankie.

Then came a snivel. Shannon petted my arm as if I'd made that sound, but I never snivel. I just privately panic.

"Get the fuck up, boy. I'm not going to tell you twice."

Something hard connected with something soft. It seemed less violent than it did…instructive.

"Okay. Okay, man. I'm up. Just hang on to your shirt."

Ricky.

Holy shit.

Each of his pathetically few words were undercut with pain, and even so, I sighed with relief. We were snug as bugs, hidden in our ditch, but instead of rocking his erection into me—Shannon's pulse swished through his veins. His heart slammed through our layers of clothing. He wasn't excited or fearful—he was furious. Any second now he might fly into a rage and leap from our hidey-hole, maybe relying on the element of surprise to save Ricky, so I clung to Shannon's hands and held on. He seemed to understand. His whiskers scraped my skin as he nodded and said, "That's the cop."

I remembered the black pits of the cop's eyes as he gazed into the Jeep, taking Shannon's measure. His neck was thick as a plug, and he had a gun.

Not good.

"So, where did your friends go?" Trooper Phelps. That was his name. He could have been the hiker on the Furnace Brook trail—and…what? He had a car waiting here? Why? Phelps wasn't about to cite us for littering or trespassing. That was no cruiser shrieking down the woodland road. It was a claptrap piece of shit. My creative mind instantly conjured a description.

Getaway car.

Something clicked—I mean other than my understanding—the Maglite.

"I...they're hurt and...I went to get help. I hit my head. I don't remember much. There was a lot of blood, but Alex...Alex Strauss. Did I tell you this? I was in an accident."

"You lying to me?" I pictured that toothpick moving as Phelps spoke.

"I'm not."

"You see anyone after your accident?"

"See anyone? Here? I don't remember." Ricky choked. He wasn't about to weep or cry. No. He gulped for air, retched, and my nose curled as vomit splashed onto the leaves.

"Oh, fuck'n hell. Don't you sick up on my shoes."

Ricky tossed his cookies for a minute or so longer. He sniffled and gagged until Phelps said shortly, "You seen my partner? He's supposed to be right here. Right in this spot," as if he were still pretending to be a cop. I bet Ricky didn't know the difference. Fear stabbed me.

That poor fuck. Ricky had no clue he'd wandered into a bad scene.

"I...I don't know. Maybe. I can't remember. I think I saw someone on the other road. We had an accident. The Jeep...it...I can't remember. I broke my wrist."

"You said." Light swept over the trees, and an owl protested with a hoot. "I thought I saw something, but it must'a been a deer. Those friends of yours run into my partner, they gonna need all the help they can get." Phelps chuckled and with a click the forest went dark again. "C'mon, college boy. Let's go for a ride, and don't you puke in my car."

CHAPTER FIVE

Phelps herded Ricky back to the car. Metal ground metal as the hinge moved, setting my teeth on edge. The car door shut. The crappy engine turned over. And over. And on the third try caught. He had a shot starter. Also, they were only using the one door, which meant he was confident Ricky's injury left him harmless and stupid. Or, given the sound of the car, only one of the doors worked.

My heart skipped as we lay inside our snug little furrow. It was a good thing we kept low, because the car didn't budge—though the headlights flipped on. Then the brights. Finally, the parking lights. Those stayed lit. Phelps skulked inside his vehicle—waiting? Sending Morse code messages with his headlights? Slapping Ricky around? Trying to text his partner? Good luck with that.

He idled in the road, and a pale beam funneled over the narrow space above us, the glowing fog shrouding us in a low-hanging cloud.

We were trapped, unless we were going to storm the car, which would be seriously stupid. I didn't even have to ask Shannon what he wanted to do, because we had to rescue Ricky from that lunatic. What we needed was a plan—other than run like hell and find a phone.

Phelps said his partner was MIA. Why would anyone in their right minds meet in Dudleytown? What were they? Lumberjacks? I dismissed the obvious reasons people trekked up here in the dark of night. Sex. Drugs. Phelps didn't strike me as a Ghostbuster or a burn-out. He struck me as a wolf in sheep's clothing.

That dude was no cop.

But the word *partner*? Cops had partners. So did businessmen. Doctors. Lawyers. And we all had sexual partners. Whatever kind of partner Phelps hoped would show, he wasn't coming, because I figured we'd massacred that dude with the Jeep.

It was black as pitch on Dark Entry Road. Cliffs and boulders the size of buses lined the road. This was Connecticut. We were lousy with ledges. Rock formations were plentiful—I'm sure Ricky could bore us to death with the geological reasons why, so it wasn't much of a stretch to imagine one wrong step sent some poor fuck plummeting.

Phelps's partner, and no shit, he meant *partner in crime* and not *pas de deux* partner—had fallen much as Shannon and I had into our hidey-hole. Only that dude hadn't stuck his landing as well.

Perfect timing, though. Phelps warned us not to take any back roads, and his bastard partner dropped like a rock straight from the sky at exactly the right time for us to nail him. *Splat.*

So where was the real Trooper Phelps?

I shoved that thought away, because the words "Prison Transport Accident" continued to haunt me.

I watched this movie on Hulu once where a serial killer disguised himself as a cop and drove around at night butchering people. He tricked women drivers by flashing his cruiser lights and then he'd pull them over on deserted back roads. As soon as one of them climbed into his car expecting safety—*wham-o*—he stripped her naked and gutted her with a Bowie knife.

Really creepy shit.

My parents think I should spend more time studying organic chemistry and less time on the file-share sites, watching bootlegged B-grade movies (and gay porn), but seriously, I've learned a lot from bad movies.

And gay porn.

Shannon grumbled, "You alive?"

"For now." I shifted, and Shannon scooted enough that I could finally turn onto my side. There wasn't much room for the two of us. My legs tangled with his, and our arms had nowhere to go but over each other. "This is awkward."

"We'll make do. We're just unbelievably lucky we fell in this pit."

"Ricky would think so." Actually, fairy holes, as we called them, were really hard to find. Usually they were covered with a soft layer of lichen—on ground that looked solid until you put your foot down. Quite a surprise for the would-be nature enthusiast when they suddenly disappeared into a hole.

I was damp as the dew slowly penetrated my jeans. I bet filth covered me from head to toe. My pants were encrusted with dirt; it was on my hands and in my hair. It was probably on my face, because Shannon seemed overly fascinated with my mouth again. His tongue peeped out, and as he wet his lips, his teeth flashed white in the night.

The better to eat you with.

I caught him looking, and he shut me out with a blink. Maybe he was considering our options as Phelps or whatever his name was, the not-cop, sat in his car. Lurking.

While I explored the landscape of my own thoughts, Shannon breathed quietly. Inside our tight little fairy hole, his arm draped over me—it should be heavy as a tree limb, but it wasn't. His palm rested comfortably on my lower back. Even through layers of clothing, it sort of burned my skin. His thigh shoved between mine, and Shannon's cock boned up again. That bulge radiated from his pants into my own hot groin, and it wasn't any product of my own imaginings when he tested the waters by nudging his dick into me.

Oh, Jesus.

Since the moment we'd fallen into this rabbit hole, I'd been tripping. It didn't matter what kind of crack Bud Lite put in their brew these days, or what power of hell tempted me from below the surface of Dudleytown, I wouldn't stop Shannon from crossing this line. No fucking way.

His fingers burrowed under the hem of my sweatshirt, seeking the tight skin of my back. When his fingertips touched me, lust shot through the soles of my feet, and I sucked in a breath. Shannon took that second to close the centimeter gap separating us. He laid his mouth on me—our first time—and I let him.

Perfect lips. Soft, moist, full. My stomach flipped as his tongue flitted to taste my lips. He moved tentatively but with experience, and his touch undid me. I didn't know if he'd ever kissed another boy, but I was willing to guess he had because this wasn't the kind of thing most straight guys do. Even the ones who fuck you don't kiss you. It's too meaningful. Too personal. Shannon's kiss was vulnerable, and so kind it scared me, but it was beautiful. I let go of doubt and licked back, tasting the plump flesh of his upper lip, his lower lip, his tongue.

Still. I had to ask. "What are we doing?"

"What I've wanted to do for a month and a half. What I think about doing all the time. What I wish you would do to me every time you walk through the door and look at me. What I hoped to do all weekend. Kiss me back, Allie. Kiss me like you mean it."

I didn't need to be asked twice. I lay my hand on his chest and lifted up enough that my hair draped like a curtain as I kissed him.

His supple lips opened, and his tongue touched me just right—not too eager, not too timid—he let me stroke in the same way I wanted to stroke inside his body, and Shannon moaned into my mouth.

"Like that, do you mean?"

I should have known better than to bait him.

"No, baby. Like this." Shannon gripped one hand on my jaw, the other around my ass, and the next thing I knew, he pressed me into the dirt and took my mouth. Totally raw, without control or restraint, he showed me how he wanted it. His tongue plunged deep inside me like a cock.

Hunger gnawed my stomach, and I shimmied to stuff a hand into his jeans. I yanked his zipper, the sound indiscernible in the night, and thank God, too. All I cared about was freeing that fat monster from Shannon's pants. Once I finally held his come-tipped cock in my fist, he was totally gone. He pumped into my fingers and said, "Help me get your pants down."

Help me. As far as romance went for Alexander Strauss? That's about all it took.

Man. I dug him something fierce.

I managed to peel my fly back and expose myself. His jeans rubbed and his zipper scraped the back of my knuckles, but his dick sought mine like an eager new playmate. Shannon let go of my rear, and his eyes never left mine as he licked his palm with the flat of his tongue. I read that as "experienced in the art of frottage and you'd better know it." My balls shriveled into come-filled nuts when he slid his spit-slickened hand over both our erections. Sure and steady and unbelievably well trained, I nearly blacked out he was so fucking hot.

I buried my nose in the thick neck of his sweatshirt, where he smelled like pine and sweat and Axe deodorant and Shannon. Oh, fucking hell. *This was Shannon.* I huffed until I was lightheaded with the intoxicating scent of man and nuzzled his prickly jaw until his mouth found mine again. With deliberate ease, Shannon bit my neck hard and proceeded to blow my fucking mind.

CHAPTER SIX

So, that was fast.

I was in recovery mode, sucking air and quaking in Shannon's arms like a wimp, when my post-orgasmic world clicked into place. The getaway car shifted gears with a rattling clunk, capping our perfect moment like a goddamn sucker punch to the head. Jesus. We'd blown loads into our pants while an injured friend sat trapped with a psycho less than ten yards away.

As priorities went, ours were pretty fucked.

Shannon's mouth left my skin. He cocked his head and listened with rigid concentration to the world outside our nook. The headlights slashed, and tires rolled over leaves and stones. As they did, my interlude with Shannon officially ended. The tiny cloud-cover evaporated, and Shannon wiped his hand on the inside of his sweatshirt. He wriggled to zip his fly. "Time to go."

"Yup." It had taken us about two minutes to jerk off—we were that supremely pent up. Well, I was pent. Shannon wasn't. He'd had sex twice since noon, making me just another conquest for the day— another successful sexual experiment.

Funny how that fact hadn't bothered me at all when I'd been humping his hand.

Man, he had rough skin and a tight grip, and when he wasn't crushing me with his weight, he thrilled me with it. My balls literally pulsed with aftershocks, and instead of pent, I was totally spent.

But now Phelps was on the move, so it was time to make ours. Shannon kept his thoughts to himself as he popped from our grave like a Halloween jack-in-the-box.

I climbed to my feet with more decorum. Actually, I staggered to my feet like a stupid D-bag. I'd broken the Alexander Strauss Cardinal Rule. *No straight guys. You can look, but you can't touch.*

Why? Because straight guys fuck their straight girls in your bed when you're in the common room studying. Straight guys break your heart—sometimes they also break your nose. Straight guys let you suck them in the locker room when the two of you are alone, but later they call you a faggot in the packed cafeteria and knock your lunch tray on the ground simply for saying hello.

That's gratitude for you.

Seriously, I'd pined for Shannon, but I'd never put myself in a position of weakness again. We hooked up in the woods. Big fucking deal. I hardened my heart, grabbed my backpack, and chalked this mutual masturbation episode up to stress and fear.

I climbed from the grave. Slivered moonlight shone weakly above the clearing and illuminated a stand of trees; their naked limbs resembled pleading hands reaching toward heaven. It was hauntingly beautiful, especially with fog hovering above the ground and fallen chimneys wobbling like ancient gravestones—as ethereally creepy as a scene from *Silent Hill*—except here a pack of coyotes yipped crazily in the distance. They turned Dudleytown anything but silent.

On the far side of the trees, the red taillights crept toward Dark Entry Road. Ricky backtracking? Unlikely he'd do that on his own.

As rocks popped and crackled under the tires, I knew where they were headed, and the thought made me sick.

Shannon had both bags on his shoulders, and I couldn't believe he hadn't dumped Ricky's load of rocks on the side of the road. That backpack wasn't exactly light. Maybe Shannon's shoulders were broad enough to easily carry the weight. "We need to follow them."

"Yup."

He gave me a cautious look, but we didn't have time for chitchat. We hardly had a moment to clean our hands.

"C'mon." Shannon trotted after the car, dead set on saving our friend. Ricky's bag rattled behind him with each footfall.

Phelps rode those brakes like a granny going to market, and the undercarriage scraped every log, pothole, and rock. That getaway car was a piece of shit. If they were serious about getting away, they'd have a plain white sedan, like my mother's Honda Accord or my sister's Ford Focus. I'm sure convicts and their peeps have to make do with what they can scrounge, but they could have at least made a little effort. They needed a car cloaked in ordinariness, not one that had all the stealth of a marching band.

Whatever.

I wished the noise of the car would drown the chilling racket of the coyotes. Frenetic yips and sharp barks echoed through the mountains, and I knew the pack had cornered something tasty.

"So what do you think?" Shannon glanced over his shoulder, and I stumbled into his back again. I hit that bag of rocks with my face and realized two things, nearly simultaneously. The first was significant.

At least to me.

Shannon deferred to me, most of the time. Not when brawn was needed and not during times of impending doom. That's when he needed to be the hero and save me—like when his hand slapped my chest during the accident, or when he'd covered me in the clearing. Normally, it would piss me off, it did sort of piss me off, but when a decision needed to be made, the fact that he asked for my opinion more than made up for the Superman bullshit. Shannon didn't tell me how things were going to go down; he didn't lay his big plan out like I was a moron. He wanted *my* input, and amazingly, he deferred to my decision.

If that wasn't a total turn-on, I mean, what was? I'm five-six and a buck thirty soaking wet. Guys don't even hear me.

Shannon did.

Here's the second thing. The man we hit was still under the Jeep. Worse, he'd become the main course for a pack of Connecticut coyotes. This conclusion wasn't one of my "lost" weekends watching old *Creature Double Feature* videos leading my imagination "astray" moments. No. Pinned beneath two tons of Jeep, lay what remained of Phelps's missing partner.

"Allie? We need to move."

Shannon always treated me like an equal, so I needed to return the favor and tell him what I knew. Ugh. He'd probably puke on my shoes.

"I know where that dude is. The one we hit. When that shitbox car stops...that bastard driving is going to see all the blood on the road, and no lie, he's going to be pretty fucking pissed." My throat tightened, and I had to swallow before I could go on. "I bet Ricky still thinks that asshole he's with is a cop. That guy's going to kill Ricky; then he's going to come looking for us because we can ID him."

Shannon nodded, but he kept walking, and I matched his pace. We'd made it as far as the cutoff to the Furnace Brook Trail, and as we backtracked up Dark Entry Road, following those demonically red taillights, the moon vanished behind the mountain. Coward.

I didn't have time to be afraid of the dark as we gained on Phelps. He rolled slowly onward as if he thought his partner might try to catch him. What an asshole—but he really could take all the time he needed, because we were so isolated in this narrow pass we were invisible to legitimate law enforcement types in the valley. No one could see us for miles.

A thin line of trees hugged a steep rock ledge. Above us, the Furnace Brook Trail ended. From the top of that mountain a person would have a perfect lookout. You could see all the way to the Catskills. It'd be a perfect place to watch for signs of police along the Housatonic River far below.

Shannon prodded me. "Right. So where's the guy we hit?"

I took a breath and spit the harsh truth out. "After he fell from the ledge and we rolled over him, we dragged him with us—and my guess is he's stuck to something, you know? A sleeve or arm or leg hooked around the axle. He's under the Jeep. It makes sense. He didn't wander off; he's skewered to that pine tree."

Shannon stared into the ravine. His throat clicked. "Seriously?"

"We saw the blood and the tire tracks, but no body, right? He's trapped. We couldn't see him in the brush." Honestly? I hadn't looked. "I didn't check under the Jeep because of all the branches, and…I wouldn't because I was afraid of what I'd find."

A severed head. Body parts. Guts. Gore. Kidneys. That's what my Hollywood-fueled imagination conjured—the real thing would be even more horrific because we were the ones responsible.

"You think he's dead? Then who made all that noise earlier? That scream. If there's a third guy wandering around, I'm going to be really pissed."

"You're already pissed. And I didn't say he was dead—or that if he was, we killed him right away. He probably came to and that's what we heard. He's had a traumatic injury—cubed. I mean look at Ricky. He only hit the steering wheel once, and he doesn't know what day it is. He still thinks that Phelps guy is a cop. That dude we hit, he's bleeding to death, and now he's attracting wildlife."

It took him a second to mull my news over, and then Shannon shuddered. "Aw, shit."

"Sorry to be graphic, but it's better to be honest." I could shoot myself for sounding exactly like my parents. "You need to prepare because it's going to be extreme."

Right on cue from the ravine, the coyotes quit squabbling and snapping.

Only a few yards from the scene of our accident, the Caddy's brakes sent a bright warning, and Shannon and I jumped the gulley and hid in the trees. He dropped the bags on the ground and, squatting, wrapped a hand around my wrist and yanked me down beside him. "What sport were you best at in high school?"

I blinked at him. "What?"

"Sport. I swam and rowed—my hand-eye coordination sucks." He said this wryly—as if I'd judge him or something. I thought his hand skills were unmatched, but I didn't say anything as he unzipped the bags and took stock of our supplies. "Allie. What sport?"

"Really? This is our conversation? There are wild dogs eating a half-dead felon, and you want to talk sports?" Shannon had finally succumbed to the mad curse of Dudleytown. "Are you sick?"

"Just answer the question."

The car idled. I could only imagine the conversation Ricky and that dickhead convict were having about the length of the skid marks gouging the gravel and all the wet shit that probably looked like blood splatter, even to the untrained eye. Somehow I felt they were more on task than we were.

"Squash."

Shannon stopped in the process of sorting the bags, and he actually choked on a laugh. "You never told me that."

I frowned back at him. "It's a very competitive sport." And professionally speaking, my parents felt squash would give me a leg up in the future. Or something. Doctors play squash, golf, and racquetball. At least, that's what they told me when they locked me inside that tiny glass room with a towering masochist in blinding white shorts. I learned the hard way just how stressful a sport named after a vegetable could be. "And I played Ultimate Frisbee—which is really awesome."

"Probably where you smoked weed too."

Not probably. *Certainly.* "Do you have a point?"

"Yes." Shannon placed a rock in my hand. It was as big as my fist—hardball sized. I stared at it while he explained. "Here's what I think—and if you can think of something better, you need to tell me right now."

See what I mean? He actually asked for my opinion. That's hot. Unfortunately, all I could say was, "I got nothing."

"Okay. So you're going to peg that fucker with a rock, and I'm going to take him down. We'll get one shot to do this because we need to surprise him, and—"

"This is your plan? *This?*" I hissed and added sarcastically, "Although, it's so crazy it just might work."

"Don't be an asshole. We need to rely on our individual strengths—"

"Did you get that from a leadership text book? Because I don't think—"

"Good. Don't think. Do."

"*Jesus.* You got that from a freaking book too."

He squeezed my shoulder, which hurt. "Yeah. Just like you with the first aid—which I need to learn, or I'm not going to graduate. We can do this. Now get in position and shut the fuck up. Once I have him down on the ground, you take his car, and we'll go."

It was my turn to latch on to Shannon's wrist. "Shan. Seriously. That man has a gun—you can't...I mean...I don't want anything to happen to you because... you know...you're too big for me to carry."

So lame.

"Then knock him in the eye." Something gleamed in his hand.

"Are you insane? A Swiss Army knife? He has a gun."

What was he going to do? Bottle-open him? Scale Phelps like a fish? Corkscrew him? Maybe Shannon could make a shank out of the toothpick and poke that cop's eye out.

The rusty door opened with a dry creak. Shannon squeezed my sore shoulder again, right before he melted into the trees.

How in the hell was I going to hit that not-cop guy with a rock?

Phelps's croaky voice carried on the wind. "Get out the car, boy." Shafts of white dome-light spilled through the yawning car door, and in it, that bastard convict looked pretty pissed.

In that same mellow light, Ricky struggled to scoot past the steering wheel.

"Move." Phelps backhanded his prisoner with the flashlight—*bam*—and Ricky went down.

Cold fury blasted me. Shannon had it exactly right. Now *was* the time to do something, and it didn't matter how I got shit done; I'd nail that peckerhead in the eye and take him down.

I slung Ricky's backpack over my chest, and with an easy grip on the rock, I took a steady stance.

"Now get your ass out of the fucking car." Phelps spat something on the ground and waited.

Please leave the keys in the car. Please let it be an automatic because I can't drive stick. Please let the car start. Please let Shannon be okay. I promise no more porn for like a week. Amen.

I took aim.

Phelps cupped his hands around his mouth and hollered, *"Chesney!"* His horrible voice reverberated exactly as expected, echoing through the hills, lilting over the canyons, blowing through the treetops. He waited, and unsurprisingly, Chesney didn't answer. "Goddamn it."

This time he faced me. *"Chesney!"*

He dropped his hands to "encourage" Ricky along, and I lobbed that stone with all my might. As that rock sailed through the air, I reloaded, pulling a fat chunk of ore or something sharp and angular from Ricky's bag.

Crack!

The first rock nailed the back window and lodged there. It didn't smash the glass as I hoped—not like Chesney's face had shattered the Jeep's windshield earlier. But I didn't let one misfire slow me. I launched my second missile while Phelps squinted into the woods making himself an easy target. That dumbass looked directly where

I stood in the cover of darkness. I could see him, but he couldn't see a fucking thing. He finally reached for his weapon, and that geologically significant stone of Ricky's capped him square in the face—hard as a rock.

I'd never hit someone like that before—we wear protective gear on the squash court—and I expected him to crumble. Instead, he lurched, his neck snapping backward with the force of the impact, but he only grabbed his face with both hands as the shadow of blood seeped through his fingers. He was stunned enough to stumble, and stupid enough not to hide. Before he could grab Ricky from the car, I hit him again. Just like in that movie they showed us in the eighth grade—*The Lottery*.

Third time's the brutal one. I reamed him in the eye. No remorse on my part. *Zip.*

Phelps screamed, and Shannon burst from the woods like a rabid grizzly bear and brought that asshole down with a flying tackle. The gun dropped in the dirt.

With his jackknife tucked inside his fist, Shannon whaled on the convict, and his big punch carried even more oomph. Smart move, because a desperate man like the one we'd taken down was gonna be hard to hold.

I dropped my rock and sprinted to the car.

Ricky lay slumped on the seat. He was pale, bruised, and bloody. His skin shone with perspiration, and puke stained his chest. His bad arm was still trapped inside his fleece. When he saw me, it hurt to watch him smile. "Hey, Alex. Sh—Shit. I—I'm really glad you're here, man. My arm hurts bad."

"I know. I'm sort of glad I'm here too." Not really, but I used my kindest, gentlest voice. I wanted to reapply his bandages and make him a real sling or something, but that could wait. "This might be the only time in the history of our friendship I'd offer you weed. If I had any. For medicinal purposes only, right?"

"Bro, I think…I'm too sick to smoke it."

"Then we really do need to get you to a hospital."

"Yeah, I'm pretty tired."

"No sleeping. Just hang tight." I shut the door.

Behind me, Phelps lay sprawled in the dirt. I snagged his flashlight from the gravel and went to find the gun. Only in a shitty script does anyone forget a firearm at the scene of a skirmish. That's just a no-brainer. I shoved the cop's stolen weapon under the backseat. And lying right there on the floor? A roll of duct tape.

"He's got a lot of stuff in this car." Ricky panted. "Camping shit."

"I'll say."

That asshole had a hunting knife, canned food, and a case of water bottles on the backseat. A Garmin charged in the cigarette lighter, and a useless cell phone blinked for service. A load of Wal-Mart bags spilled onto the car's floor. The duct tape? He probably used some on the real Phelps earlier. I bet that Cornwall cop was a good guy, too. Just doing his job, keeping the peace, and writing tickets. Paying his bills, and making the town safe. He'd be nothing like that pile of feces Shannon had pinned to the ground.

Shannon.

Blood had taken its usual toll on my roommate and he gulped and swallowed from his position in the road. He might have the constitution of a little girl when it came to medical horrors, but he'd sucked up his fear and gotten the job done. Actually, he was kind of amazing. A real-life action hero.

Our prisoner verged on consciousness, so I strapped his hands and feet together with the shiny tape. I added a strip over his mouth because I didn't want to hear any bullshit when he woke—which he did now. I left him squirming in the dirt, tossed the roll in the car, and said, "Holy shit. We did it."

A total fucking miracle.

"Yeah. Well, you did. I can't hit the broadside of a barn. That was effing unreal." Shannon ruined his compliment by gagging after he checked Ricky. "O'Leary. You might have to move over, 'cause I don't know if I want to puke or pass out."

Ricky said weakly, "Just do something so we can get out of here."

"I'm on it." Shannon peeled his Tri State sweatshirt over his head, and his T-shirt molded to his chest. I shouldn't notice, but it was impossible not to. He was a tawny-haired, hazel-eyed, outdoor-leadership Adonis. He panted in the night air, his breath fogging, and his slim waist and broad shoulders captivated me. He embodied the word "tapered."

God.

My mouth dried as he scrubbed the blood from his hands with the come-stained jersey.

I'm so sick.

Shannon nodded at Phelps and said to me, "Let's go—we can lock him in the trunk."

Actually, that wasn't a bad idea, but first? I glanced into the ravine. The pine forest below grew still as death. Only the wind and the rumble of the car's motor chased away the silence. "You know we need to go down there and look."

Shannon spoke directly to our duct-taped hostage, "Just sit there, and I won't hurt you."

That was kind of ironic.

The man couldn't run, couldn't speak, and the look he leveled on us? Madness. Hate. Evil. My skin crawled as I remembered all those people who died right here in Dudleytown where the sun didn't shine in the shadowy pass of these three mountains and the wind blew without cease. That stupid curse. The lightning strikes. The murders. The rampant insanity and all those poor souls gone missing.

Oh, whatever.

I'd seen this movie plenty of times, and I knew how this story ended. When all was said and done, we were the good guys. We'd walk away fine.

Shannon clapped my shoulder, and I shrieked and clutched my chest. "*Jesus*. Don't freak me out like that."

He frowned over the abyss. "I know one of us has to climb down there and look, but why don't you wait here—"

"Don't be stupid. We go together if we go at all."

"Okay. Get the keys and I'll load him in the trunk."

I snagged the key ring from the ignition, and the engine stalled with a sputter. Ricky uttered his first coherent words all night. "We're screwed if this car doesn't start again."

"C'mon, loser." Shannon dragged Phelps around the back fender by his shirt collar. The man's ass scraped the ground, but he took one look at the trunk, and the dude went bonkers—shaking his head and rolling his eyes and fighting like a wild thing until he fell over in the dust.

I couldn't help myself. I said, "Maybe he's afraid of the dark."

That pussy.

I stuck the key in the lock, and as Shannon wrangled our fugitive, the trunk banged open with a pop—exploding like my bag of chips had earlier. A man, *a grown freakin' man*, naked, white with cold, and zip-tied at the wrists, sprang from the back of the car like one of those circus snakes in a can. He took me down, and I smacked the gravel with a spectacularly painful fall. I looked into that determined stare and almost crapped myself. Whoever he was, he wanted to kill me. He raised his tied hands over to club me—

"Trooper Phelps!" Shannon snagged the man's wrists with his powerful grip. "Sir. We're not going to hurt you. We're friends, and we're here to help."

Eyes round, I nodded mutely.

Like everyone else but me, Phelps was a big man. Not only was he ripped, he was freezing to death. His shoulders shook. His skin prickled with cold. That poor dude had been trapped in the trunk waiting for this one moment to charge his way to freedom and, wow, we'd saved this cop's life.

That tidbit would go on my résumé.

Shannon ripped the tape from Phelps's mouth—the real Phelps—and used the Swiss Army knife to free him.

"Thank you." The cop's voice shook in time with his shoulders. "I thought I was dead...I...I can't believe it."

The sound of loose rock falling and gravel kicking down the road alerted me. Trooper Phelps pulled Shannon's dirty sweatshirt over his head. Headlights swung around the hairpin, and miraculously, a parade escort of three patrol cars rolled down Dark Entry Road one after the other.

Shannon handed the half-naked trooper a pair of sweats from one of the packs and sighed. "It's about fucking time."

CHAPTER SEVEN

Back in Goshen, I'd been in the house safe and sound for ten minutes when my relieved parents left to buy us a celebratory pizza. No shit. They were impressed, but they were also realistic. And they were hungry. Shannon disappeared into the spare room to change. I closeted myself inside my old bedroom and checked the dresser mirror. I looked like crap.

I stripped my nasty clothes, and...I saw the bite.

Fuck. He'd bit me!

I slapped my neck, but I still couldn't cover that monstrous bruise. And everyone had seen it. My folks, the cops, Shannon. *Ricky.* That loose-lipped blabbermouth would tell everyone we knew.

Actually, Ricky probably wouldn't remember.

The last thing Ricky recalled of the entire evening was making that fateful turn onto Dark Entry Road. Hours later, shaken and confused, he'd balked at going to the hospital with the uniformed strangers until I explained they had good drugs and free HBO. He could stay the night for observation, watch *Game of Thrones*, and get bombed without having to drive home.

The paramedics carted Ricky away, and Shannon and I waited while the cops searched the ravine for leftover chunks of Carl Chesney. The coyotes had made short work of him. It seemed beyond sick to whisper *the dingo ate my baby* to Shannon, but those words wiped the look of horror from his eyes, so I was glad I did it.

Exactly as I reasoned earlier, Chesney fell from the ledge. The cops speculated that he'd gone to the lookout to wait for his partner—the flashlight-wielding Geoff Martin. Off to ditch the stolen cruiser, the plan was for Martin to carjack the first sucker who drove by. Which turned out to be us. When that Connecticut State Trooper flew past us on Route Seven with his blue lights flashing, he'd scared Martin into scurrying back up the hillside.

The trooper had saved our lives. We were one for one with the Connecticut State Police.

I had a pancake-sized love bite, and Ricky in his "right mind" would have blabbed my business all over the dorm—or worse, tweeted it across cyberspace. Ricky's injury saved me from being the butt of a dorm-wide joke. What kind of friend is glad for a mild case of amnesia? I mean, honestly.

I stared at my neck. *Shannon.* Those moments had been so thrilling. Who knew he'd turn out to be part vampire?

Then I noticed something in my hair. The pale strands were clumped together with dried blood. I had blood on my forehead. Blood on my jeans. And dried come on my clothes and in my pubes.

Gross. In one evening, I'd turned into a walking PSA for *Men at Risk.*

I should take a shower, but I continued to stare at my skinny self for a minute longer. My blueberry-blue eyes blinked boyishly back.

Face it, Strauss, you had sex with Shannon Murray. This is not a drill. Now what are you going to do?

Hide.

Straight or not, he'd been a great roommate. A good guy. He made me laugh. He bought me beer. He was kind and good-looking, and he never freaked over having a gay roommate. No. He sort of liked me actually, which was astonishingly PC of him. I couldn't imagine Ricky offering me the same welcome.

Shannon Murray stuck up for me. He trusted me. He valued my opinion and laughed at my awesome jokes. We had conversations, and he never bitched about my movie obsession or about sleeping with a light on. I couldn't wait to see him every morning when I woke and every evening when I went to bed. Every time I opened our dorm door and saw him studying, sleeping, hanging around—my heart flipped. And he kissed better than anyone I'd ever locked lips with.

The truth was, I loved him. Had loved him since day one.

How could he be such a jerk and fuck someone else in my bed and still be so amazing? Unless Shannon could be the same person in public as he was with me in private, I couldn't be with him. Case closed. I may have enjoyed his come on my stomach and his mouth on mine, but there wouldn't be an encore. I couldn't do it. Never again.

I'd have to switch dorm, and that fucking sucked.

Knuckles rapped on the door, and speaking of things that sucked, Shannon slipped into my room. One look at me standing in my boxer briefs with my hand to my throat and my hair sticking crazily around my head, and he grinned. He'd wet-combed his own hair away from his forehead. He was free of leaves, scrubbed clean of dirt, but his knuckles were pale and raw. He'd dressed in a tight blue T-shirt and a fresh pair of jeans, and those feet? Bare.

He checked me out from my toes to my hair, and those too interested eyes didn't miss a speck. I probably looked like I'd just stepped off the orphan train. I felt like a perv. Dirty. The worst sort of dirty.

Come stained and porn dirty. *Do me*, dirty. He was dressed and I was naked, and that's pretty much the plot for half the movies I watch.

Please don't let me get hard now.

Shannon seemed amused by my hickey and tight underwear. I didn't throw him out because, you know what? I wasn't going to pretend that episode in the grave never happened. I wouldn't play that game anymore. We'd had sex. He could deal with it, or he could break my nose and knock my lunch tray to the ground. Time to get real. "I can't believe you bit my neck."

"You weren't complaining at the time." He shrugged and dropped his backpack. "My teeth marks kinda look good on you."

I'm pretty sure my jaw unhinged.

He unearthed a white sock from the depths of his bag and waved it. "Don't move."

Half a second later, Shannon draped that tube sock on the doorknob and with a smack, he shut the door.

I blinked. "Are you out of your mind?"

"You told me to do this. I'm simply following orders."

"My parents will see this." I flung the door wide, grabbed his sock, and chucked it at him. *"Asshole."*

"I was kidding, Allie. I wouldn't have left it there. Relax."

"Relax? We're not hooking up, Shan. I'm taking a shower."

I was halfway to the bathroom when Shannon's voice stopped me. "We'll see."

We'll see? That was uncomfortably erotic. Six two and burly, he hulked across my bedroom, and my stomach fluttered. How could I be this pissed *and* this turned on?

Easily. I even lusted over his great big toes when they stopped inches from my smaller ones.

"I want to make a few things clear before you have time to jump to any more stupid conclusions."

"Stupid? Me?"

"Yes." He smiled. "You." His irises were flecked with the same tawny-brown pigment of his hair. I stiffened as his warm arm tucked around my back and hauled me into his chest.

"What the fuck are you doing?"

"Experimenting."

"Back. The. Fuck. Off." I wriggled to free myself, but Shannon held tight. "Look. Maybe you think I'm some kind of novelty act, a sure thing to blow you or something when you feel the need, but *I* don't experiment anymore. I don't have to. I know who I am."

Sort of.

"Hey." Shannon squeezed. "I'm kidding. I'm not experimenting either. I know who I am too. And I know that right now I want to feel you right here against me."

I pressed uselessly against his pecs. His nipples pebbled into my palm, and his cheek brushed my hair. I stank, and he smelled charmingly of my sister Karen's shower gel, which was a little sexually confusing. Shannon's skin brushed mine, and my too-willing dick plumped up like an extra-long Ball Park frank. It nudged his crotch.

Oh, so what. I'd jerk off in the shower if I needed to. I wasn't doing this again. "That's nice, Shannon. Move. I need a shower."

"You got that right. Man. You reek. C'mon." He snagged my hand, and I stared at our clasped palms. "Your room is huge. You have your own shower, right?" For once, Shannon didn't hear me, didn't ask my opinion, and didn't wait for me. He looked around, found the bathroom door open, and dragged me inside. "We can take one together."

"One what? Are you high? Did Ricky dose your chocolate milk? We're not fooling around."

"Why? Give me one reason." I yanked my hand, and he let go, but only so he could turn on the faucet. Water sprayed onto the tile in a downpour. He spun the knobs, and fog formed. Shannon checked out my tiny bathroom like he was considering moving in. "*Lord of the Rings.*" He nodded at the Aragorn wallpaper. "You're such a nerd."

Steam whistled from my ears. "A reason? Okay, I'll give you three. You're straight, you're my roommate, and you were with someone else *today.* I don't think witnessing your blowjob in my bed is jumping to any conclusions. Just so we're clear—I don't screw guys that pretend to be things they're not. Not anymore."

I dropped my underwear, half-mast and all, and climbed into the spray. Hot water poached my shoulders, and within seconds dirt and worse circled the drain.

Shannon's voice rose over the curtain. "Just because I'm not as courageous as you doesn't mean I'm not gay."

Courageous? Me? I blinked soap away and let that slide. "Gay? You? No fucking way."

"Why? You don't own the gay experience, Alex. Everyone is different. Every single person has his own story. I haven't told my parents yet, but I want to. I will. Otherwise—it's not a secret. I was giving you space. I didn't think—"

"You are so full of shit." I shampooed my hair furiously—and my heart skipped helplessly with something that felt like hope. Or disbelief. Maybe those two emotions were intertwined.

"What do you have, a meter? A piss test? A litmus test? I'm two years ahead of you. We don't run in the same circles. I'm private and I don't fuck around. Ask O'Leary. He knows. He gave me shit all night. Weren't you listening? He knows I wanted to be with you. And I didn't have sex with that girl, she gave me head, and...I only enjoyed it because...I thought she was you."

I dropped the soap. If Shannon were in the shower with me, bending over might hold the same promise it had in some of my favorite movies.

No. That Bunion chick had sucked Shannon off and he'd enjoyed himself. I'd seen them. "If that's true? And you used her? It's sick. It's not okay. That makes it like ten times worse." I thought for half a second while rinsing. "Not that I'm a misogynist or anything. Girls are fine. But...I'm not one of them."

The curtain slid on metal rings, and Shannon, naked as a jay and hard as a telephone pole, climbed in.

I didn't cover my crotch with my hand, but I wanted to. "Get out."

His hands rested on his hips. His jaw tightened. "No, you dumbass. I was sleeping. I jerked off in your bed because I wanted to be with you so bad I couldn't fucking take it anymore. I fell asleep."

"What?" *What?* Shannon had jerked off in my bed?

That was so wrong. And so not-Shannon. So bad and so...fucking on.

Warped by years of internet porn, my nimble young mind pictured him masturbating in breathtaking detail, mostly because the detail was standing right in front of me. His erection waved from a thatch of brown pubic hair—angry and alone. His cock craved attention and a warm, wet place to hide.

I licked my lips.

Water ricocheted off my shoulders and sprayed onto Shannon's chest. His skin glistened. His eyes glimmered.

He took the soap from my hand, and muscles rippled everywhere. "You must have walked in between me enjoying it—because honest to God I was dreaming—and that moment when I wasn't enjoying myself because she thought the whole thing was a joke. She thought she was funny knowing I'm in love with someone. Like it's okay to make me the butt of her sick joke, but it's not."

I blinked. I blinked and really, truly saw him. Shannon stood naked in front of me, hurt and embarrassed and offering me the whole truth.

I touched his arm. "It's not a joke to take advantage of someone, ever. I'm actually…man, I'm sorry. What a bitch."

We were brothers in arms or something in our shared humiliation. People suck sometimes, I swear to God.

Soap bubbles dripped as he slathered his chest and worked his broad palms down his abs. He made me crazy with his sliding slippery hands.

Shannon scrubbed. "She snuck into our room, and when I woke up, someone was sucking me. I stopped her."

I quit staring at his dick. "But you said it was an experiment."

"Well, I did…wait…like a few seconds…I mean, it wasn't…I didn't know at first."

I rolled my eyes. "God. No wonder you were so pent up in the woods."

"I've been pent up for weeks." Shannon let the water sluice the lather away. He set the soap on the shelf. I waited, and he didn't disappoint me. "All I want is to be with you."

"Honestly, I've heard that before, Shan. From guys a lot like you."

He snorted. "Doubtful. There isn't anyone like me."

I laughed, and the second my guard let down, Shannon snagged my wrist and crowded me into the tile.

"C'mon, Allie." My shoulders met the shower wall, and he tipped my chin back. Water pearled in his hair and beaded on his eyelashes. A hot stream gushed over his shoulder and swept between us. Slippery and wet, our erections touched.

His voice dipped huskily, "All I know for sure, whether you believe me or not, is that I am crazy in love with you. I have been for weeks."

Love?

"What? No, you aren't."

"Yes." His slick arm slid around my back. "I am. I love everything about you. I love how you leave a light on at night when you sleep. And I love how you pretend your homework is so difficult, but you put your headphones on, and the more you get off on solving some problem, the louder you hum." His lips touched my neck just above the bite. Heat unfurled in my stomach, and my knees wobbled.

"I do not…"

Holy crap. I do hum when I study.

"I love how you take four sugars in your coffee, but you tell everyone you only use two." Shannon's lips flitted across my jaw, and I lifted enough for him to lick a path to my ear. His breath was minty. "I love the way you bite your lip when you choke up. You do it when you come too. I've seen you."

"What? Where?"

He bit my ear. "Tonight. And when you're in the shower. You do it a lot too."

His fingers whispered across my nape, and he kissed the side of my mouth.

"I love that. And I love how, even when you're afraid, you stay calm when life turns to shit. You did that tonight. You deal. You think. You get the job done, and you're always, unfailingly kind. You're going to make a great doctor."

Talk about a direct hit. That nailed me.

Water rained on us, and Shannon's hands glided across my skin as if he was getting to know me. I had a feeling he really was. I held on, touching the smooth length of his spine and the gentle slope of his ass. His smiled crookedly. "But when you compare life to a cheesy movie—that's the best thing. I love that so much. Have you ever seen *Boys & Bears*? Or *College Dorm Suck-Off 2*?" He breathed into my ear, "Those are my favorites, Allie. And they're yours too."

"You watched?"

"All the time. It's all I could think about when we were hiding in the trees."

I fucking panted with lust as Shannon Murray slid to his knees right in front of me. Oh my *God*. He'd been watching my porn, and now, he planned to make fantasy come to life. I mean, if that isn't love...

Shannon Fucking Murray is gay—and he loves me.

My dick pulsed, and Shannon's hungry tongue lapped across the head. "Oh, fuck *yeah*." I latched on to his hair. I think anyone else would close his eyes and do something feeble and dreamy, but screw that gentleness crap. I never in my life expected anyone to get on his knees and service me. I wasn't about to miss a second.

Shannon held the globe of my ass in one hand, and the other steadied my dick. His perfect mouth finally shut up, and he showed me the fucking money.

He pressed me into the wall and gobbled my cock—dipping his tight lips and eager mouth over the length of me with finesse. Up. Down. Sliding and suckling until I squeezed handfuls of his hair and that first ripple of fury unleashed inside me. Wet. Tight. Soft. I probed the depth of his spectacularly capable mouth, and when he took it all, I knew my roommate had given plenty of head before.

Even more pornographically hot, Shannon made noise as he blew me. He effing loved it. He fucked me out loud until I cupped his neck and came in a wicked, head-spinning rush. My knees weakened. My pulse swished. My breath stopped. The entire universe shifted, and my heart exploded.

Shan-non. Shan-non.

Come blasted from my nuts, and I shot hard. I cried out, and Shannon soothed my hip. The sound of him swallowing was the best thing I'd ever heard in my life.

It took a few minutes of nibbling and licking and kissing my crotch before Shannon climbed to his feet. I couldn't move. I just blinked at his knees. They were spotted red. He didn't care; he just rinsed his face and smoothly shut the water off.

Flopped against the shower wall, limp as my dick, I wanted to thank him. Wanted to say something. Instead, I kept my mouth shut.

Shannon smoothed my hair back, and when he kissed me, I tasted the ocean—salt and sea. "You can say it now, you know. Because I know you love me too."

I did, but fear made me cautious. "You won't walk away when I enter a room? You won't pretend this never happened as soon as we get back to school? You won't go downstairs tonight and eat my parents' pizza and act like I'm a stranger? You won't ignore me, or... because I can't handle that again. I'd rather not say anything at all if your plan is to walk out of here and treat me like shit."

My words were tight and way needier than I intended. Shame stained my face.

"Hey." Shannon held my jaw, and his eyes gentled. "Never. Ever. You can trust me. I trust you with my life. I promise you, we're a team. We're together. I love you."

"Okay." I nodded like an idiot. Why couldn't I find the balls to say what I need to? *I love you, man,* wouldn't cut it.

"We could have died tonight, Allie. I think we deserve this. We deserve each other."

He needed to hear the words. He'd taken such a risk, too, and I did love him. His faith never wavered as he waited, his hand loose, water droplets chilling on our skin.

I went for a joke. "We might never leave the dorm room again."

"That's fine with me."

So I swallowed, bit my lip, and the words I wanted to say for weeks finally tumbled free. They were quiet. "I love you too."

Man. Love took way more courage than facing any terror Dudleytown had to offer. Hand to God, my heart almost burst from my chest, crawling out like some half-starved *Alien* baby, it lurched so desperately. It needed so much.

"This is going to be great. You'll see." Shannon smiled, squeezed me, and drawing my *Lord of the Rings* shower curtain aside with a snap, he said, "C'mon man, I'm starved."

SIMPLE GIFTS

A CORNWALL NOVELLA
by L.B. GREGG

To my darling Rosie

CHAPTER ONE

I fled the Sharpe family's unbearably merry Christmas with my coat undone and my head bare. A battalion of inflatable snow globes hovered on the front lawn, and here on the lakeside of the house, a wicked wind blew shrapnel of ice across the shore. Tiny shards flayed my cheeks, but I still chose frostbite over that stifling scene inside the house. Easily.

From the moment Sunny pried me from her idiotically small car, I knew I shouldn't have come. We'd pulled into the vast circled drive under a ring of oak trees, and I'd gaped at the Sharpes' stately new second home like the orphan I was. "Isn't this where they filmed *Home Alone*?"

"It's a little much, I know, but my Dad thinks it's necessary for the election."

"I can see why." The brick fortress epitomized *Members Only*, much as the senator did. I smoothed my tie and checked the buttons on my wool overcoat.

"My mom's expecting us." Sunny smiled weakly. "I don't want to upset her. She's got her hands full with all this."

I swiveled, trying to take 'all this' in at once. A mammoth choo-choo train spun its flashing wheels on an imaginary track beside the front walk. Santa grinned from the engine. Eight spherical snow scenes stood in formation by the hedgerow, wobbling in the wind. When we passed a pair of mechanical reindeer genuflecting to the grass, I couldn't keep quiet. "Jesus."

Sunny waved a mitten at the side yard. "Asleep in the manger."

She stopped at the front door and took a steadying breath. Mascara made her eyelashes a mile long tonight, and those deep, dark eyes were Anne Hathaway huge, but the line of her mouth gave her away. I'd known Sunny Sharpe since we were dorky outsiders together in the eleventh grade, and I knew this look.

Fear.

"Hey." I tucked my hand into her mitten-covered one and gave her fingers a squeeze. "Everything's going to be all right, Sun."

"I hope so." Sunny squeezed back. The wind gusted across the lawn, and her shoulders shook.

"Ready?"

"*No.* Wait. I have something to tell you. Please don't be mad. I should have told you as soon as I knew, but I was afraid you wouldn't come tonight, and I thought you should be here. You belong here."

Dread's icy finger touched my heart. She took a deep breath. "Robb's home."

The bombshell hit me hard enough that I dropped her traitorous hand and took a step back. "Are you *kidding* me?"

"I know! I should have warned you. I'm sorry! I knew you'd cancel, and I couldn't stand for you to miss out. I don't want you to be alone."

"I've been alone since I was six. I like being alone. What the hell, Sun? Way to blindside a friend on Christmas."

Robb Sharpe. I'd carried a torch for Sunny's tall, dark, and handsome older brother since the day I arrived in Cornwall as a bumbling sixteen-year-old. Having come from one disastrous foster situation, I landed smack into my last equally disastrous placement. I'd had a bad haircut and cheap sneakers, and on the day Robb and I met, tongue-tied and painfully self-conscious in the presence of Sunny's God-like big brother—swim team captain, student body treasurer, mathlete—I'd fallen down a flight of stairs and landed literally on top of his feet.

Oh my God. He's home.

At least he wasn't dead. Although, at that moment, I sort of wished *I* was.

"Robb's here?" His name tasted of longing and shame. I choked that shit right back down where my feelings belonged. Buried. "Now? Tonight?"

"Yes. I'm so sorry!"

"Shit." What was I doing at the Sharpes' Christmas party anyway? I knew better. I'd never come before, why change my plans this year? I glared at my sweet-faced friend, then searched the cold brick mansion for a glimpse of dark eyes staring from behind the glass. Light twinkled from every window, but there was no sign of Lt. Sharpe. I didn't see him. That didn't mean he couldn't see me.

The trees groaned. Wind whistled across the lake, and the snow globes jiggled like Jell-O. I shivered inside my coat. "You're absolutely sure?"

"Yes, of course I am. I should have told you."

"You should have." I swore I'd moved on. Not *geographically*, of course, but I'd come light years from the needy kid Robb had left behind.

I could just die. But I wouldn't.

"Don't frown," Sunny said automatically. "You'll get crow's feet."

"Nice. You sound exactly like your mother." I rolled my shoulders and did my best to smooth my features, but too late. "I'm fine. It's fine. We're good. I'm good. Let's go."

"You are more than good; you're great."

"Nice pep talk, Tony the Tiger." My watch read seven o'clock. In a perfect world, I could get in and out of this nightmare in twenty minutes if I tried. "Let's say Merry Christmas to your folks and then I need to get back to the bar."

"Okay. Thank you. Chin up and smile."

"Spare me."

She squared her shoulders, slapped my back, and shoved me through the black lacquered door. Inside, the house smelled like old money—balsam pine, scotch, and beeswax. The air buzzed with party noises. A curved stairwell led to a gallery on the second floor where an enormous crystal chandelier gleamed overhead. When a thin woman in a starched apron took our coats, I knew the Sharpes had truly entered a new realm.

I shoved the problem of Robb right out of my mind and checked my tie in the mirror. "Where's your mom? I should say hello to her first."

"Jase. Where's your blazer? Did you leave it in the car?"

"What?" *A jacket.* "I…*Oh my God.*" I froze at the threshold of the formal front hall. Decked appropriately in velvet and lace, Sunny stared worriedly at my chambray shirt and flannel tie. "*Who the hell goes to a Christmas party without a coat?* I can't go in there now. Drive me home."

"No! Forget I said anything. You're fine. And I love this tie." I slapped at her hand as she tightened the knot. "It's okay. I doubt anyone will notice."

"You noticed."

"I'm in retail. I notice every detail. Plus, my mom loves you; she won't care what you wear, just that you're here."

"You say that now."

"And Robb's an adult with his own problems. Honestly. He'll probably just say hello and clam up. He's really quiet."

"He'll say *'Hello'* in a coat and tie. I know it."

"I think he's wearing a sweater, actually. And Robb's got other things to deal with. My father invited a few lady friends for him tonight. I have no idea why."

"What?" I stopped fiddling with my tie. "Robb's gay. Even the senator knows."

"It's hard to explain, but when Robb arrived a few hours ago, my dad insisted. Talk about having issues." She blinked her big, brown eyes, and I softened. Damn her. "Don't leave, Jase. Please? For me? I don't want you to be alone."

"But I like being alone…"

Sunny yanked me through the threshold, and we were in. She gave me a quick tour of the house as if I wasn't hiding from a ghost. I must have hidden pretty well, because I never saw Robb as we passed garlanded doorways and into walnut-paneled rooms brimming with tipsy family members and well-turned-out neighbors. Every man in attendance wore a freaking blazer or a cashmere sweater. Sometimes both. And always with a tie. There must be a rulebook I wasn't aware of.

Sunny eventually faded into the depths of the house with the promise, "I'll be right back," and I found myself alone. A long table piled with platters of Christmas goodies stranded me. I fortified myself with a whiskey-laced eggnog and picked at a plate of curried meatballs. I didn't interact with another guest until a curvy woman in a raspberry-colored dress sidled beside me and spilled wine on my shoes. "Oops!" She stumbled away giggling as I stared at my soaked loafers.

Why am I here?

I folded a linen napkin into the form of a dove and set it on the table next to my empty cup. Time to brave the crush in the living room. Time to get out and get back to work at the bar where I belonged.

I needed to thank Mrs. Sharpe before I fled, so I scanned the room for Sunny. Interestingly, not one person in our age bracket—the under thirty and still single crowd—was present, with the exception of a stiff-looking man guarding the mantle. Two sleekly dressed women flanked him.

Robb Sharpe. Holy hell, he'd been standing a few feet from my nose the entire evening, and I hadn't recognized him. Gaunt and raw-boned, he'd aged ten years, easily. Time had stamped lines on his face and something, maybe experience, hardened him.

Robb observed the party as if sent here to gather intel and report back to the front lines, but he ignored the two women so pointedly, I knew they were the senator's invited guests. If those ladies were looking for a good time, they needed a better map.

I stood in the doorway gathering my courage, struggling to find the right words. How could I possibly bridge a gap of ten years with a simple *"hello"*? *"How are you?"* seemed trite. *"Hey, it's good to see you,"* too revealing.

"Jason! Where do you think you're going?" Sunny's willowy mother intercepted me with a smile. She pulled me into a light hug that smelled of cinnamon sticks and alcohol. "You haven't even said hello! You can't leave yet."

"It's getting late." I squirmed inside her embrace, patting her bony shoulder with an awkwardness born of embarrassment. In my book, public hellos and goodbyes should be offered at arm's length, but Mrs. Sharpe didn't let me go. She hugged and squeezed, her hair tickling my nose, until she finally looped an arm through mine and walked me into the very center of the crowd.

"I was just saying to Freddie how nice it is to see you."

"Me?" She must be tipsier than she looked. I'd seen Frederick Sharpe working the crowd of registered voters at the bar. He barely offered me a glance, never mind a word or a handshake.

Mrs. Sharpe patted my arm. "I'm so glad Sunny brought you. She always said you don't like Christmas, but I never believed her. Everyone loves Christmas."

"Well, you know how Sunny can be, so here I am."

"Yes. Here you are." She smiled again. Her lipstick had faded over the course of the evening, but her skin glowed from too much Merlot. "And so handsome too. Is that a new tie?"

"Same tie I always wear."

"You look like a movie star."

I'd been told that on more than one occasion. Blond, blue-eyed men have a strange effect on women of all ages.

Mrs. Sharpe's eyes widened. "You know what? You should join us for Mass."

Mass?

"Tonight?" I choked and checked over my shoulder. Robb still held the mantle in place, a beautiful woman hanging on either sleeve. He looked like I felt—ready to bolt.

Mrs. Sharpe laughed. "I meant tomorrow night. For Christmas Eve."

"Oh. Right. Thanks, but I really should leave before then."

"To do what? You should stay with us for Holidays. We'd love to have you." She walked me across the broad living room as if she wanted to parade me past her son. "But, just in case you can't stay, I have a little something to entice you."

"I hope it's your daughter. She promised to drive me home tonight."

"Oh, you can't get away that easily." Mrs. Sharpe glanced at her son and gave a tiny ladylike cough. "Did you say hello to Robb? I know you were good friends when you and Sunny were in high school. He could use some friends now that he's home."

Friends? A blush crawled from my collar to my neck. "I haven't had a chance yet, no."

"But you will." She nodded. "Promise?"

Robb drank from a can of soda, and his opaque eyes took in our stroll. I couldn't tell if he was watching me or his mother or the wall, but I could guess. The heat prickling my skin climbed higher. I had no clue what to say to him, or to his mother, but I had to say something. "I will. I promise."

"Good. Tonight's the first time we've been together in years. It's going to take some getting used to."

"I understand." I had zero experience with family relations, so my words were merely polite.

That seemed to be enough for Mrs. Sharpe. She squeezed my arm again. "I'm glad you decided to come. You should stay the rest of the week. Have Christmas with us. We can go skating and play broomball—have a real New England holiday. I hate the thought of you being alone."

"I'm fine, and Riley's can't run without me. But I appreciate the invitation."

"Just promise me you'll think it over."

"Sure." We arrived at the library door where an enormous tree filled the room. Cocooned in finely spun angel hair, and crisscrossed with strands of bold lights and flimsy strings of popcorn, the fragrant pine floated above a sea of tastefully wrapped gifts. It looked exactly as a real Christmas tree ought to—only more so. Wooden toys, ceramic birds, and shimmering bells weighed every branch. Round glass ornaments hung from the boughs. The tree-topping star could have guided the Magi east.

"Wow."

"I know. Christmas is what I do best; however, I lose all sense of proportion during the holidays. Maybe Sunny warned you?" Mrs. Sharpe winked before turning to dig through the pile of loot on the rug. "Now, let's see…I have something here for you."

"For me?" I almost asked her why, but I sealed my lips and settled my feet.

Mrs. Sharpe straightened and dumped a bulging Christmas stocking, complete with a striped candy cane poking from the top, into my empty hands. I hadn't had one of these since…well, *ever*. I squeezed the velvet until the sound of crumbling paper stopped me from strangling the thing. She'd written my name in glittery cursive on the cuff. Handcrafted, like I was family or something.

But I wasn't family. No family of mine had ever given me a scrap, unless you counted the one-way ticket to foster care.

Yes, Sunny and I always exchanged gifts. We were friends. This year, I had a new book on astronomy, and I'd given her a silver hedgehog charm for her bracelet, but a gift from Mrs. Sharpe? I was practically a stranger to Sunny's parents. Probably the gesture meant nothing—maybe she gave presents willy-nilly to every constituent who entered her palatial lakehouse.

But, damn, her gift meant something to me.

My throat closed, and I swallowed against a rising tide of emotion.

"Merry Christmas, Jason." Mrs. Sharpe said gently and, alcohol-afflicted or no, she seemed so fucking sincere I had to look away. Robb's quiet stare met mine from across the room. He saw right through me. He always had. Heat reached my hairline. I broke free of his gaze and squinted down at my overfilled hands. *You knew better. You knew not to come.*

My eyes blurred.

I had nothing in return for this woman. Not a bottle of wine, or a grocery store poinsettia, or even a lame greeting card. A plate of cookies, for Christ's sake. I could have made a paper chain for her tree. Something. Anything. I hadn't even come properly attired.

There should be a handbook for orphans. Honestly.

Mrs. Sharpe waited, her eyes soft.

Damn Sunny all over again. She could have given me a heads-up about this too. She knew I'd arrived here like that pitiful Drummer Boy from the song. I had nothing to give. And I hadn't offered a single word of welcome to Robb.

The shame that had stolen my tongue as a child returned, but I managed to keep things real enough by eking out a simple, "Thank you."

"Oh, you're very welcome, hon. We're glad you came—and if you'd like to stay, please do. We've plenty of room, and we'd love to have you." She gave me another squeeze, rumpling the present between us, and when she let go, the second after I wrinkled her dress with my sweaty orphan palms, I fled.

I nabbed my coat, located the nearest exit through a jungle of ele-phantine pink poinsettias, and hit the Sharpes' narrow sun porch at a goddamn trot. A zillion festive white lights lit my way until I passed through that dazzling portal to a silent, frigid night.

I sucked sweet air into my lungs once my feet were safely on the porch and clutched the collar of my coat, then tucked the stocking under my arm. Pinpricks of sleet bit my cheeks, but at least there weren't any Sharpes here—only a howling gloom that whistled over the frozen waters of the lake and shaped the fallen snow into long, spiny hills. Lights flickered on the north shore. Or maybe that was Old Saint Nick himself headed this way.

Maybe he could give me a lift back to town.

The stars were hiding. A bulb hung from the boathouse, spilling yellow light onto the overflow of cars. A path bisected the snowdrifts and ended at the boathouse door where a snow shovel rested against the batten boards. Shadows flickered in the second-story windows.

I buttoned my coat and trod to the porch steps, literally an outsider on every level. I *knew* better than to intrude on a family during the holidays. Not because I wasn't wanted in some peripheral way—I'd turned this invite down for ten solid years. But this year, Sunny had snagged me by the arm and trundled me into her perky little car, hoodwinking me with her fake encouragement and her false cheer. *"You have to see the new house! Please come, please?"*

I shouldn't have come, because I didn't belong. That would go in the orphan handbook, because these weren't my people. Jason Ferris had no people—just a cat named Norm and an apartment decorated with folded bits of paper over a town bar I owned outright. Not much of a life in the grand scope of things, but it was my life. I'd built it myself. I belonged there.

Snow blew through the yard, punctuating my solitude. I wasn't afraid of being alone—I didn't know anything else. But a fleeting, intimate moment in the house with Mrs. Sharpe? That terrified me.

Cold nipped at my knees, urging me to slide along the path in my slick-bottomed party shoes. I aimed for the boathouse. I needed a ride home, even if I had to go by sleigh. I couldn't walk eight miles to Cornwall Bridge. I wasn't that desperate. Not yet.

As I hunched into the gale, something flashed across the lawn. A sphere bound into the sky, twirling like a giant carnival balloon. It bounced onto the shoveled path and bells jangled. "What the hell...?"

Another ball bounced off the porch and sailed by, narrowly missing my head.

Those tacky, inflatable snow globes. They'd come loose from their moorings and now wobbled chaotically toward the driveway as they deflated. Another ball ricocheted onto the lawn. Flying balls. They sort of cheered me, and I laughed for the first time all evening. What an unexpected pleasure to find at Senator Sharpe's house. The snow globes jiggled crazily across the snow, driven by the December wind. Poor Mrs. Sharpe. She'd have a cow tomorrow morning when she found lifeless balls on her meticulous lawn.

"Jason! Heads-up!"

The impact forced the air from my lungs as a blur of smooth, black plastic bowled me over. My head hit the icy ground with a sickly, hollow *smack*, and a tunneling void swallowed me.

CHAPTER TWO

A voice like broken glass yanked me from the deep. "Hey. Wake up. Can you hear me?"

Cold seeped from the ground and leached all the warmth from my bones. My head pounded like a motherfucker, but my ears worked fine. "Yeah. I hear you."

Snowflakes kissed my face. They were angels' tears, or reindeers' tears, maybe. I thought I heard bells ringing from across the lake.

"Hey. C'mon, Jason. Open your damn eyes."

"Yeah. I'm awake." Five more minutes and I'd get out of bed. Just five…more…

I drifted.

"Jason. Open your fucking eyes. It's snowing on your face. Get up. Get moving." He shook my shoulder with a bear paw of a hand. "Let's go."

"Okay." I opened my eyes and snow swirled above me, falling like paper confetti. A pair of grim, white faces hovered. They bore a striking resemblance to Lt. Robb Sharpe.

"Good. You're back," they said.

"Back? Did I go?" My mouth felt funny. Why was I sleeping on the ground? The entire Sharpe clan would frown on my peasant-like behavior, but pain pinned me in place. White light exploded inside my head, and when I moved, stars danced behind my lids. "Holy shit. Did you hit me?"

"What? *No, I didn't hit you.* Thanks a lot. You've had an accident and whacked your head." Robb bent close, kneeling with a crunch of ice. His expression remained unchanged from earlier. Not a hint of the kindness he once possessed softened this guy. Or guys. I had double vision.

A penlight appeared from thin air, and I shielded my face. "Hey. Not cool."

"It's okay. Let me check your eyes."

"They're blue."

"Yeah. No kidding." A ghost of his old smile appeared, stiff from lack of practice. *Now, that's an improvement.* "You cleaned your clock pretty good, and you're bleeding on my mother's Frosty the Snowman."

"Did I deflate it?"

"Flat as a pancake. Happy Christmas. You're using it as a pillow."

"That explains my headache." The light disappeared, and I blinked into the whirling snow. "What happened to your voice?"

"Smoke inhalation. That's what had happened. An accident. We'll talk more later."

"You sound like Harvey Fierstein."

Robb peeled off his parka before barking to someone over his shoulder. "Start the truck. Crank the heat."

"Truck? I don't think I can drive. Is it stick?" A chill wracked my limbs. "Man, it's freezing."

"Jason. Focus." Robb draped his coat over my chest, and his body heat saturated my senses. I latched on to that warmth as I had the frigid air earlier. His parka smelled of down and pine. "Can you wiggle your toes?"

I could. "My toes are fine. It's my head and—I need to get up." Pieces of the accident came together, but a new disaster loomed. Nausea forced me onto my right side, and I fought against a flood of eggnog, meatballs, and curry. What had I done? What was wrong with me? "Give me a second." My teeth chattered, and I bit to cover the sound.

All business, Robb waved his hand inches from my nose. "How many fingers do you see?"

"Two. No. Four."

"Two. Congratulations. You have a concussion."

"No, I don't. I'm fine. I'm just winded."

"You're a lot of things, Jase, including clumsy, but winded doesn't make this list. If you need to puke, now's the time. Better here than in the truck. We need to move."

Move? What was he expecting? Mortar fire? "I can't believe I've been taken down by one of your mother's lawn ornaments."

"You were. You cracked the hell out of your skull. Good thing it's thick." Robb shifted and behind him, a field of onlookers popped into my vision like cartoon characters. Sunny and her boyfriend Lyle—*pop pop*—the Sharpe twins Ana and Jane—*pop pop*—and a few stragglers I didn't know. I didn't see the senator—*thank God*—but voices whispered from across the yard.

I would keep my supper down if it killed me. I wouldn't puke for this crowd, or Robb. Not in any scenario. Of course, I'd sworn I'd never fall on Robb's feet again in this lifetime either, and here I lay.

A pair of Tory Burch party shoes stepped in front of my nose. Sunny crouched beside her older brother, and side-by-side, with their short black hair and matching deep-set eyes, they still looked more alike than the twins. Her wooly mitten stroked my cheek. "You okay, Jason?"

"Fine. Aren't your feet cold? Where are your boots?" My feet were freezing. "Can you drive me home? I'm sort of partied-out."

"You do look a little beat, but let's stop by the hospital first. Okay? You smacked your head pretty hard. I heard the ice crack all the way inside the house. And now you're bleeding on my mother's balls."

I couldn't even laugh, that's how bad I felt.

"Bleeding?" I touched my scalp gingerly, and my fingers came away wet. My stomach roiled anew. "How bad?"

She bit her lip. "Not too bad."

"You're lying to me again? Right now? Seriously?"

"You're not bleeding to death or anything." She pressed something against the back of my head. A frown creased her forehead. "You're fine."

"Great." Sarcasm took energy I didn't have, so I closed my eyes and didn't open them until the truck's tires crushed the snow ten feet from my Frosty the Snowman bed. A tunnel of white fog floated above me.

Robb stuck a meaty hand under my armpit. His bare fingers circled my sleeve, and his left arm slid around my back. "On three; you ready?"

Was I ready? A half dozen Sharpe faces peered over the porch railing, watching my sickly progress. Icy sweat formed above my lip, and my belly soured again. "Yes. Let's get out of here."

"Roger that. Here we go. One. Two. Three." The world tipped back to center as he hauled me to my feet. I swear to God, every drop of blood in my body drained straight to the soles of my feet, except for the real stuff flowing from my scalp and wetting my collar. My vision tunneled, my head swam, but Robb Sharpe held me by belt and shoulder. What a way to reconnect. "The sickness will pass in a sec. You're fine, just a little hypothermic. Take a breath."

Pass. Please pass.

When had I turned into such a squalling infant? I'd been hurt before. I'd had a hundred stitches on my thigh when I fell down a ravine in the seventh grade and stuck myself on a pine tree. I'd had my appendix removed, my tonsils snipped, and God knows, I'd had my heart ripped out. I could handle a simple blow to the head.

As Robb promised, the nausea and vertigo faded, and my vision cleared. He didn't drop my arm, he held fast. I let him. "Let's move."

"Sunny," Robb barked at his wide-eyed sister. "Call 'em and tell 'em we're on our way."

"Isn't she coming?" I didn't see her leave, but her footsteps retreated. The wind blew my hair as he stuffed me into the warm cab and, in another second, Robb climbed behind the wheel. With a shift of his hand, we backed onto the driveway.

I caught a quick glimpse of Mrs. Sharpe's pale face and Sunny holding a cell phone to her ear as we took the driveway at bone-jarring speed. "Really. I'm much better now."

I spoke to myself, of course, because Robb didn't say a word. I held the dash with one hand, and with the other palm, I pressed some scrap of cloth to my head. In the mirror, my pupils were huge and my golden hair matted.

"You're okay. Those cuts can bleed, but they're usually nothing. You need your head stitched. I offered, but my mother said it wouldn't do. Not in the house."

He couldn't do what? Lay me on the kitchen table next to the beef Wellington and sew me together with a trussing needle?

In that fleeting second of disbelief, I remembered something vitally important. *Health insurance.* I had none. I barely had a dime in the bank to cover expenses, and certainly, I didn't have enough nickels squirreled away to pay for something as frivolous as a visit to Sharon Hospital.

I nearly asked him to give me the home repair job, but I wasn't going back inside the Sharpes' lakehouse come hell or high water. So, I closed my eyes and let him drive.

CHAPTER THREE

Robb clammed up the second I signed a *Discharged Against Medical Advice* form, so the world was white noise and white snow on the walk back to the car. There was nothing to say anyway. He drove, and I stared at the road while painkillers dulled my mind. The nausea that threatened me earlier reasserted itself every time he turned the wheel too fast, but I managed. I couldn't afford a stay at the hospital. Not to be observed for thousands of dollars I didn't have.

I hadn't said much to Robb, and in my own defense, he didn't seem to mind.

We passed Cornwall's white clapboard church, the snow-covered cemetery lined with crooked headstones, the one-roomed Post Office, and, at the end of Main Street, Riley's—my bar. The lights were burning, and the place looked busy. I should be there, working my tail off and earning my mortgage payment. Two stories above my business, a lonely apartment waited in darkness. I pressed my nose to the passenger window as we drove past.

I should be there.

Wishing wouldn't make going home any more likely. That wasn't part of the deal I agreed to when I signed the DAMA, so I buried my disappointment and let Robb drive me toward my worst nightmare—A Holiday at the Sharpe McMansion.

Colorful lights whizzed by in a blur, and the last glimmer of Cornwall faded from the rearview mirror. I made one final stab at autonomy. "I feel much better."

"Save it." Robb croaked and stuffed an empty coffee cup into the cup holder. He squinted through the windshield, and by the dashboard's glow, the black stubble covering his head made him look a little like a Chia Pet. "I promised my mother and Sunny I'd keep an eye on you. This was your choice."

"Right, but I'm only staying one night. We agreed."

"We'll see how you look tomorrow. The old man thinks you might sue him—he may insist you stay."

"He should let me go home, then. I can't sue him if I'm dead." Christmas with the senator? Honestly? I'd rather slip into a coma.

Robb shot me a look. "Not funny. I've seen head injuries take a turn for the worse more times than I want to count."

I believed him. Something dire had happened to Robb—probably recently, given the purple shadows under his eyes and the deep lines fanning from the corners of his eyes and bracketing his mouth. He'd lost a lot of weight, his cheeks looked hollow, and his voice? Absolutely ruined. That might explain his silence.

We drove through thickening snow. The Housatonic River snaked blackly on one side of Route Seven and the forested hills of Cornwall towered along the other. White houses hugged equally whitened lawns, and somewhere beyond Coltsfoot Mountain, the stars hid their pale light.

I gripped my discharge papers—which consisted of a dire list of *what to watch fors*—and while those papers made tonight's sleepover at the lake necessary, they didn't make the stay any more palatable.

Sunny would be at her parents' house, but she had her own life. And, of course, she had her new life, with Lyle.

The paper blurred, and I blinked to clear my vision. I'd become a burdensome thirteen-year-old again, trucking toward another home where I didn't belong, nothing more than a charity case. A misfit. All I lacked was a paper sack of clothes on my lap and an overworked social worker at my side.

I smoothed the wrinkles from my discharge sheet before making the first, clean fold down the center, just like old times. Leaning into the headrest, I worked without a plan, folding and creasing from memory until the sprightly form of a reindeer revealed itself in careful paper pleats.

Voilà. Origami reindeer. If only I could make a team of them and fly myself away.

I set the piece on the dash. "Rudolph will guide the truck tonight."

Robb gave Rudolph a flat look and shook his head. "Man. You haven't changed at all, have you?"

I couldn't tell whether the idea pleased him or disappointed him. Still, I cringed. "Actually, I've changed in more ways than you can imagine."

"Really?" The noise he made resembled a cough more than a snort. "You fell at my feet earlier, and now you're making origami animals. It's like the last ten years never happened."

Fell at my feet earlier. Well, hell. "You do remember."

Robb gripped the wheel. His stare didn't waiver from the road. "Of course I remember, Jason. I was eighteen. I'm not the one who got hit on the head. I remember everything."

Everything? I envisioned Robb's younger self, his rough hand slithering inside my jeans, his mouth hot on my neck, and his long hair brushing my cheek. *Don't think about sex, no matter how earth shattering that sex was.* I cleared my throat. "You didn't act like you knew me earlier."

"Yeah, well, right back at you. You walked past me how many times? Not even a glance. Nothing. Not a nod, or a 'hey, nice to see you.'"

"I didn't recognize you. You're..." Gaunt wouldn't sound nice. "You look different."

"You look exactly the same."

We hit a bump, and the fragile paper reindeer fluttered to the floor. Robb's hard jaw clicked shut, and tension filled the cab, smothering the air inside like a blanket. Since the radio didn't work, the only relief came from the sputter of the fan pushing heat through the vent.

He turned onto an unpaved road, and rocks banged inside the wheel wells and pinged around inside my bruised head. "Can you maybe take it a little easier?"

"Hang on. We're almost there." He eased his foot off the gas, and I cut him some slack. Because of his mother's rogue snow globes, the man had missed his family reunion, even if his only enjoyment came from standing alone, back to the mantle, frowning past tittering lady friends. His first time home in years and the family didn't radiate joy over his homecoming. They tiptoed around him. I'd seen them firsthand. Still, I didn't need The Handbook for Orphans to tell me some gratitude on my part was in order.

"Thanks for driving me to the hospital."

"Why? Total waste of time. You should have stayed. I don't know why I'm surprised. You were always that way."

"What way? Poor?"

"No. Determined to do things on your own. The second things get real, you sever ties, run and hide."

Floored, I gaped at him. Robb had been the one who'd run fast and far, not me. Unless he counted tonight. "I'm just saying that I appreciate you leaving the party on my behalf. That's all. Thank you."

"I should probably be the one thanking you." His jaw clicked shut. A vein throbbed on the side of his fuzzy head, and despite my irritation, I wanted to know what the hell had turned him into such a dick. Maybe he deserved standing alone all night.

Or maybe he preferred standing alone. I know I usually did. Maybe he'd become more like me. Maybe he was hiding too. His parents sort of acted like they wanted him hidden.

"I should have said hello. You're right. I apologize. Glad you're back. You look good."

"I'm not back. I'm visiting. But sure, you too. You look good, I mean." His eyes never flickered in my direction. Apparently, *good* meant *invisible* as well as *the same*.

"Your mom's happy to have you home." Not that I had much first-hand experience with what made mothers happy. Mine had left me alone in a hotel room just before my sixth birthday and vanished into thin air.

But if I had a mother, a *normal* mother like Robb's, unlike the host of foster mothers I'd known over the years, and if I'd risked life and limb for my country, I imagined my mom would shout the news of my homecoming to anyone who'd listen. She'd have finally untied her yellow ribbon from the old oak tree and waved it around like a victory flag. She'd have grabbed on to my sleeve at that party, and she'd never have let go.

She'd ease my way, reintroducing me to friends and family alike, making me the center of her attention.

Robb and Sunny's mom hadn't exactly done that. I knew she loved him, she seemed concerned about him, but she'd kept her distance, leaving him in the company of a couple of tipsy, chesty, "friends." She'd spent her evening sampling the Merlot and focusing on the other guests, including me—a nobody.

Shit. She'd also given me that embarrassingly sentimental gift. "You didn't see a Christmas stocking with my name on it, did you? When we left the yard? I had it earlier."

"What?" Robb looked at me like I'd lost my marbles, and medically speaking, I probably had.

"Never mind." I frowned. "I guess your dad's happy you're home too. I mean, except for the part where he wanted you to spend time with his lady friends."

Robb turned his stunned gaze in my direction. His jaw swung. "*That's* what Sunny told you?"

"Yeah. She gave me a head-up when I got there." *She probably worried I'd embarrass everyone by throwing myself at you again.*

He slapped his forehead. "This is why I can't live in Cornwall ever again. My family interferes with my life, and I have zero privacy."

"You had more privacy in the army?"

Ignoring my question, Robb squinted over the dash. "Did you know I was at the house?"

"Not until I walked through the front door. I had no clue. Sunny didn't tell me."

"*Christ.*" Robb yanked the steering wheel hard to the right, and the truck slid onto the shoulder in a spray of gravel and ice. I grabbed the dash as my stomach lurched and my head reeled.

"What the—?" I glimpsed through the back window. Red light reflected on the snow. "Are you out of your fucking mind?"

"Yeah. Indisputably." Robb set the emergency brake, and *bang*, he exited the vehicle and vanished into the opaque forest.

Tree limbs clawed at the sky above the road, and a whirling dervish of snow howled across the road. "As God is my witness, I am never going to another Christmas party as long as I live."

I wasn't going to chase after him either. I hadn't then. I wouldn't now. Mostly because if I fell on a patch of ice, I'd be in that hospital so fast, my credit cards would explode. I couldn't risk it, so I waited for my deranged chauffeur to reappear, while the flatbed filled with another layer of white. Snow sizzled against the windshield. The windows fogged, and the chill settled. In the densely wooded forest of Cornwall, Connecticut, houses were few, and the blue night closed in.

I'd been through worse.

And clearly, so had Robb. He'd spent his first evening back in the family fold looking like he'd rather face a firing squad, not that I blamed him. And the Sharpe clan had sort of ignored him—which made Robb more of an outsider in his own home than I was.

Some vital piece of information eluded me. Something I couldn't put a finger on. My drug-addled mind pondered the possibilities. Maybe Robb preferred women now. Our fling could have been a folly of youth—or a phase. Stranger things had happened. Straight guys got horny and had sex with gay men all the time. Young men experiment. Robb looked straight as an arrow to me now. More so than before. Actually he looked straighter than ever.

But he wasn't. I'd stake my business on it. *Lift up, Jase. Up on your knees. Oh yeah, fuck yeah. Just like that. I promise, it'll only hurt for a second.*

That liar. I'd hurt for years afterward.

I stuffed my chilly hands into my coat pockets, but cold seeped in from every crack. Minutes frittered by until the door popped open and icy air dusted snowflakes onto the driver's seat. A frosted Yeti climbed inside. Robb's stubbly head hid under a funky wool hat. Braided flaps hung past his ears, and he looked years younger.

Somehow, I managed to keep my voice even. "You okay?"

"Peachy." The engine roared to life and blessed heat blasted from the vents, but Robb didn't put the truck into gear. He white-knuckled the wheel. His shoulders hugged his neck, high and tight. "Just forget that happened. Sorry."

Ice crystals glistened on his hat and melted on his eyelashes. A droplet rolled down his cheek like a tear.

I needed to clear the air or get out and walk. "This entire evening has been one disaster after another. And the painkillers are making me say stupid things. I didn't mean to offend you. Seriously. I'm not good at reconnecting. Or connecting, for that matter."

"You didn't do anything wrong." He clipped each word. "You're fine. Except for your head. I didn't think seeing you would qualify as a disaster. I'm sorry for that too."

"I didn't mean seeing you. That fell more under the heading of *unnerving* than anything else."

He ground his teeth and blinked wordlessly through the windshield.

"Look. I have a headache, there's a blizzard brewing outside, I'm tired, I'm freezing, and no shit, I want to go home to my own bed and sleep. So pretend we're strangers—"

"We are strangers."

"No, we're not, but if that works for you, fine. We're strangers. If you have something you want to get off your chest, you have a captive audience. Literally. And I'll put anything you say in the vault. Actually—I am the vault. I always was."

Snow piled on the truck's hood. Inches of fresh accumulation covered the road, blowing in gusts that wafted across the head beams. The heater's fan squealed, and my stitches pulsated. I managed to keep my mouth sealed, giving Robb time. Eventually, he cleared his injured throat and said, "I can't go back."

"Back? Where? To the Army?"

"Yes." His hat dripped, and he wiped his cheek with the heel of his hand. "And no. That's over and done—I thought you knew."

"No. I—I'm sorry. I didn't."

I tried to remember how long he'd served, and how long he'd been deployed, but Robb kept talking. "I don't want to go back to the house. I can't deal with my family."

"That makes two of us. Are you pissed? I'd be pissed." I think I was pissed on his behalf, actually. They'd provided female companions for their gay son.

"Of course I'm pissed. I've been home, what? Six hours? They act like...they're embarrassed I've come home."

"So why did you come? You never have before."

"Because..." His voice trailed off, and I felt a lie brewing. "I promised my mother. I didn't know my father would hire a babysitter for me. Two babysitters. If Sunny knew beforehand, she could have given me a heads-up."

"You and me both."

Robb frowned. "I was leaving when you fell. If you hadn't been leveled in the yard, I'd be gone."

"Gone? You just got here. Where were you going?"

"I hadn't thought that part through. Somewhere. Anywhere. Away."

Who's running now? He didn't blink as he watched me from across the cab. In his ridiculous hat—the thing smelled of wet sheep—he looked more like the old Robb. The one I used to know. Strong. Reliant. Real.

"I knew I should have stuck with the original plan and done Christmas by phone. My family works better long distance."

They certainly couldn't hurt him from afar. "How long distance are you talking? I'd say some family close by is probably better than no family anywhere, if that's what you're used to."

"Yeah, well, I can only pretend for so long." Robb flung his Yeti hat onto the dash. Icy water slid down the windshield and adhered to the wiper blades. "I couldn't believe you actually came. I thought you hated Christmas."

"I don't hate Christmas. Why does everyone think I hate Christmas? I don't like family get-togethers, but Sunny begged me to come." She'd insisted. She'd done so because she wanted me to see Robb. And Robb had wanted to see me.

Now that he was sitting beside me, I was sort of glad I'd gone, head injury notwithstanding. Robb Sharpe and I had always made a weird sort of sense, the weirdest, and God knows I could talk to him. I just couldn't trust him.

I chewed on that while Robb unzipped his coat and dialed down the heat. The squealing fan slowed to a low-pitched whine.

One thing became crystal clear to me as the seconds ticked by—*I could go home. If Robb chose to, he could come with me, in a strictly* platonic way. I had a couch. He'd fit if he didn't mind his feet hanging off the end.

"We should go back to Riley's." I cut him off before he could object. "Tell your mother the roads were bad, or tell her I puked in the truck. Tell her you have a flat. Tell her I fainted. Or, we could tell her the truth and say you want to stay the night with a friend."

A yawn ruined my plan as the pain medication kicked in. I could manage my headache and my stitches, especially with my head resting on the seatback and my eyes closed.

"Friend, huh?"

"Friend. You can sleep on the couch. Make a decision because I'm wiped."

"You look like shit."

"Thanks. Great bedside manner, Dr. Sharpe."

"I'm not a doctor. Not yet." I raised my eyebrow at that bit of news. Robb whipped his sadistic penlight out again and did his best to blind me. "Let me check your eyes."

I snatched his wrist. "Please. Knock it off. I'm totally fine. The doctor said so."

"No, he said—"

"I took three painkillers. Hand to God. Can we go now?"

"Are you going to puke?"

"Not unless you don't start driving."

The threat of vomit pushed Robb into action. The penlight disappeared, and the wipers shuddered before scraping ice across the windshield with a squeal. Snow slid to the hood. This ride would be tough no matter which direction he chose because all hell had broken loose outside.

Robb buckled his seat belt and put the truck into gear. "Hang on."

We fishtailed onto the lake road and, *fuck yeah*, he swung the truck around, and we made a beeline back toward Cornwall.

"Thanks."

"Yeah. We'll probably regret this."

The road turned into a whiteout as we chugged slowly along. My lids drooped, and the heat inside the tight cab made my limbs feel boneless. Before I closed my eyes and sank into sleep, I placed my paper Rudolph back on the dashboard. "Guide our sleigh tonight."

CHAPTER FOUR

"Jason. Wake up. We're here."

"I'm up." For the second time tonight, Robb Sharpe shook me awake. I took a bleary look out the truck's window, and a treacherous mix of snow and sleet fell in the amber streetlight in front of the bar. Christmas lights twinkled around mullioned windowpanes. A chunky wreath hung from the door. *Riley's Tavern.* I probably should have changed the name years ago.

Despite how welcoming my place looked, when Robb killed the engine I couldn't move to go inside. Those painkillers had me by the short hairs.

The passenger door opened, and a snow-shrouded Robb held the door. His goofy-looking hat was back in place. "Let's go." I tried to climb from the truck, and my loafer slid. He caught my elbow. "Careful. Sidewalk's slippery."

His breath made puffs of cloud in the air and, maybe I was stoned or dreaming, but he had more energy than I'd noticed previously.

I shook the cobwebs from my brain. "I'm fine. These shoes are slick."

"Just don't fall on your head, or you'll bust it open for good."

We shuffled across the sidewalk like two old geezers. Tree limbs glistened overhead. Weighted power lines dipped across the street, spelling disaster for tomorrow's last shopping day of the season. Ice glazed the wrought-iron railings. Robb held my coat sleeve well after we'd climbed the steps and left the night air and crackling wind behind us.

The shovel and pail of salt I'd left in the portico earlier stood unused. I tried not to let that piss me off too much. As we entered the warm vestibule, the smell of draft beer and French fries made my stomach flip. *Welcome home.*

"Hey, Jase," my right-hand man Donnie called over the crowd. I needed him to clear the steps, clear the house, clear the dishes, and handle *everything*, so I choked back my irritation and gave him a nod. Donnie moved nimble and quick, seamlessly serving beer and pretzels and taking cash, but his gaze hovered on my coat sleeve until I shook free of Robb's grip.

"You good?" Robb croaked. I guess the smoke inhalation left him incapable of whispering because his next words echoed across the bar. "Where's your bedroom?"

Every head in the joint turned.

I knew those people and never, not in all these years, had I brought a soul back to the bar. Not a fling or a fuck or an overnight guest. I didn't entertain men at home. I didn't bring any guests home. I hadn't had a friend upstairs in five years—except Sunny—and she'd only been inside my apartment a handful of times.

My privacy had been hard-won, and in some ways, it was all I had.

"Jason? You good?" Before he could dig that intrusive light from his pocket and torture my pupils for the hundredth time, I moved away, albeit slowly.

"I'm fine. Donnie, can you clear the steps before we get sued?" I kicked the snow from my shoes and pretended to be "fine," but the heat must be set too high—the place sweltered at sauna level. Every pair of eyes watched me, none more carefully than Robb's. I'd left my ruined shirt inside a trashcan at the emergency room, and now my borrowed hospital shirt itched. I tried to act normal, whatever that meant. "How's everyone tonight?"

Smiles, waves, and a chorus of "fine, great, Merry Christmas" echoed, but not a single comment regarding my matted hair or my intense new guest.

"How're the roads? My car buried yet?" Pete Nester gripped a coffee mug and stared balefully at the contents. He should have gone home an hour ago. The snow must have kept Mrs. Nester from retrieving him. "Gonna walk home."

"We're gonna slide home on our asses," someone said, and even I laughed.

"Time to go." Robb barked and flipped the television off. "Bar's closed." Jaws dropped, but he either didn't notice, or he didn't care.

"Who the hell are you?" Pete asked as Robb dumped the contents of a full coffee pot down the bar sink.

"I'm an old friend of Jason's and that"—he jerked a thumb at the sleet and snow hammering the window panes—"is some serious shit." He pocketed his silly hat, hung his parka by the door, and took control of my business with a single glance. "No last call. Drink 'em or lose 'em."

I offered a lame, "It's really coming down," and every patron bent an elbow.

Robb took in the ancient dartboard, the flat screen TV, the faded athletic photos of townies who'd come and gone over the last fifty years, and the gold-painted name over the window. He put his hands on his hips and gazed back at me from the old mirror above the bar.

He actually smiled when he said, "Looks the same as when Coach Riley owned this place." *I remember everything.* "Glad you didn't change anything. Riley's really suits you."

Robb's kindness absolutely rattled me.

"He saved my life," I said, and with those words, I stripped myself bare.

Gabe Riley had taken me under his wing when the last living situation of my adolescence soured. He'd put me to work, me and Sunny both. The two of us had cleared dishes inside and sneaked beers outside in the alley that entire summer after our senior year. The same summer Robb graduated from college and disappeared for good. When Sunny went on to Amherst, I'd been left behind. "I didn't want to change things. As sort of a tribute."

"Great guy. He coached my swim team." Not the same thing at all, but Robb marched on to the next topic with another croaking call to the locals. "Hats and coats people—Riley's is closed. Move out."

I would have added *"Merry Christmas"* or *"drive safe"* or *"please don't slip on the steps,"* but after hours of silence, my cell phone sprang to life. I answered on the second ring. "Sunny?"

"Are you okay? Where are you? I can't reach my brother! Is he okay? Did you guys have an accident? Did you kill him? Was he a jerk? He didn't try to sew you up himself again, did he?"

Mrs. Sharpe's frantic voice drowned any background noise. "Ask him if they're on their way. How's Jason's head? Is Robb behaving? Is he okay? Tell them to drive slowly."

Jesus Christ, I'm surrounded by them.

"Jason," Sunny said, so firmly she practically channeled her brother. "Where are you?"

"Calm down. I'm fine. We're at the bar. The roads are bad, and we're stuck here for the night."

"The night? Well, lucky you. I'm stuck here."

Mrs. Sharpe said, "Sunny. I can hear you."

"You call getting five stitches lucky?"

"I do if you're at home, and I'm at the lake. You have no idea," Sunny breathed into the phone.

Robb cleared the bar of drinks, empty or not, then hit the dimmer on the overhead. The lights blasted my eyes, burning brighter than the sun. I turned the lights down and went to silence the Christmas music.

Donnie grabbed a coat and ran for the door. "Just going to go clear those steps for you, Jason!"

"Good call," Robb muttered.

Once inside my murky office, I leaned against the door for privacy, and squeezed my eyes closed. I just needed a second to—

"Are you still there? Why are you so quiet?" Sunny's voice permeated my consciousness. "Jason? Are you okay? Where's Robb?"

"Sunny. For God's sake. I'm fine. And I told you, Robb's here. He commandeered the bar. He kicked everyone out, and he's closing. He's a hard-ass, but a very capable one."

"That's him. Capable. At all costs. He's also a dick who won't answer his phone and, uhm, someone here doesn't like being ignored." Mrs. Sharpe chimed in, but Sunny spoke over her, "You're really okay? Mom said you left the hospital without the doctor's approval and that Robb is your guardian angel. She's not happy. *I* should have gone with you. I'm more angelic than Robb any day. I'm so sorry. My brother split before I could get into the car."

I tread with care. Something about having Robb here with me instead of Sunny, my closest friend, felt right. "It's a small truck, Sun. Better for you to be at the lake, with your parents."

"Now you're just being mean." She snorted. "But you're really okay? No fracture or anything?"

"I'm fine. I have a cut and a bump. No big deal." Spots floated behind my eye, and a yawn popped my jaw. I needed to get upstairs to bed or sleep there on the floor. I could have used the chair and desk, but my bed was softer, and my cat needed attention. "Everything worked out for the best, and now I have a medic on call in case I rupture an aneurism."

"You're not funny."

"I gotta go. I'll see you in the morning."

"Promise?"

"No. I have to work. I have a business to run."

"*Fine*. I'm so sorry. For everything. I should have told you." She whispered, "But I can't believe Robb's staying with you. In your apartment. Alone. *Overnight*."

"There's not much I can do about it, is there?"

Mrs. Sharpe mentioned something else. "Okay. Okay!" Sunny said. "Mom wants you to know she has your Christmas present, and she cleaned the blood off, and you have to come by tomorrow. She won't hear otherwise. Her words exactly."

"Great. Tell her thank you. I'll do my best. Now I really need to go."

"Wait! Don't worry." She snuffled into the receiver as if she held it too closely, and I knew she didn't want her mother to overhear. "Jason. Robb's seen a lot of things…really awful things…and he's changed. Okay? Just remember that. But inside? He's still the same guy you used to know. He wanted to see you. And I promise, you can trust him. I do."

"I'm not worried," I lied easily through my drug-induced haze. I'd been too tired and concussed earlier to consider the ramifications of Robb physically *in* my apartment, alone, with me. But as I pocketed my phone and considered Sunny's words, her anxiety spread like a catching disease. Fortunately, the office door popped open, and Robb knocked some sense into me.

"You ready to go? Your guy Donnie's closing shop." He barely glanced at the office as he bullied me toward my apartment door. "Power will cut off in the next hour or so."

The lights flickered as if he'd ordered them to. Freezing rain pecked at the windowsills in the back hall. I unlocked the door, and we entered a chilly hallway, leaving the heat of the bar behind. I led Robb to the third floor on worn stair treads that creaked underfoot. Weak light illuminated a cluster of cobwebs, and I squelched any embarrassment. I don't like to dust. Also, I had bigger troubles ahead.

Damn Sunny all over again. *Now* I was worried.

I'd lived in this building since the fall after high school graduation, when I'd been promoted to bartender. Long before he sold me Riley's—on payment plans and percentages and prayers—he'd let me move into the upstairs apartment, offering me a place of my very own.

Robb clomped at my heels. What would he think of my apartment? *He'll think you're just as much of a fruitcake as ever.* Sure, he may have wanted to see me, but maybe he'd change his mind once he got a look at the real me. My furnishings were meager, and the walls were painted a joyful sky blue, but it was the collection of paper sculptures, and the—

"Is there a problem? You're awfully quiet, and you're dragging your feet. Are you dizzy?" He joined me on the landing. A window faced the alley, where lights from the center of town glowed orange through the snow. My apartment door waited, so I found my keys.

I stalled.

"Jason? Everything okay?"

"Yeah. Fine. Quick question. Do you like astronomy?"

"What?" Robb closed the distance between us, and I caught a whiff of spice, pine, and wool. He reminded me of a lumberjack, not a soldier. He'd left his parka down in the bar, and his sweater sleeves were pushed to his elbows, his shirt collar lay open, and the sight of his pale Adam's apple had me biting my lip.

His finger brushed the back of my hand, and I fumbled the key. Sick or nervous or not, the fleeting contact snapped across my skin like an electrical shock. His touch thrilled me.

"Jase?"

I stared at his fingertips, familiar yet strange, and the air between us shrank until I couldn't breathe to speak. Honestly, with a single stroke, he robbed me of thought.

I pulled away, but he said, "Hey. It's okay," in a disturbingly husky voice that I recalled too well. He took the key from my palm, and I almost fell down the goddamn steps. I wanted to bolt—living up to his expectations—but he grabbed my borrowed shirt in his fist, and my heart fluttered against his knuckles. His breath warmed my cheek. "Steady."

Mother. Fucker.

A smile hid inside the rough tones of his broken voice, and the sound eased my troubled mind while stimulating other less troubled areas. I knew that voice. I'd heard it before—in the dark of night, in the backseat, under the stars, in the boathouse, in his bedroom, behind the bleachers. And I'd hear him say *steady* again in the dark tonight, as I lay alone in my cold bed.

And, *bang*, I knew why he wanted to see me. *He still wants me. He hasn't let go, either. He came to see me.*

I would have stumbled a second time, but Robb had me. Jesus, he had me good. "You need to lie down."

I really, really did, but I could not for the life of me move to unlock my own front door.

"You good?"

"Yup. Fine." I squeaked, and he let me go. Robb fit the key into the lock, and I stifled a groan.

What the hell kind of drugs had they given me at that hospital? I swear I'm tripping.

The sound of my apartment door swinging free sobered me. "No, wait! My cat—"

In a flash, Norm vanished into the stairwell, but that was the least of my worries.

"What the hell…?" Robb blocked the doorway. "Holy crow. Are those *stars*?"

I froze at the threshold of my home, not that Robb noticed. He wandered in, face tipped heavenward to better see the strange beauty of my apartment's contrived night sky. Above his head, paper starlight shimmered down from a black-lit galaxy. *Orion, Sagittarius, Ursa Major, Canis Minor, Scorpius, Gemini*—the constellations hung in painstaking precision, glowing on purple pinpricks, lighting the darkness.

Accurate and overly detailed, I'd crafted every star, made each scrap of paper, and creased every fold. The project had taken years but, voilà, origami universe.

Robb wandered, and the stars led him through the apartment, straight toward my bedroom as if they guided a wayward captain home after years at sea.

I shook that idiocy from my head, and on leaden feet I trailed after my overnight guest. Hot blood colored my cheeks. "I know my apartment is a sort of odd."

"No." He turned to look at me, and I banged into his chest. "Did you make all of these?"

"Well, yeah. Who else?"

"I swear, the sky looks exactly like this in the desert. Clear and wide and the stars go on forever. Only not as colorful, or so close." He tapped a tiny pointed star, and it spun on a delicate silver thread. "This one was done in pieces, right? How the hell did you make them so small?"

"Practice." I left him marveling over my freakish masterpiece and flipped the bedroom light switch. There were a couple pair of jeans on the floor, and the simple maple bed lay unmade, but otherwise, a portion of the Milky Way flowed from my window, over the bed, and disappeared in the closet. Pretty much business as usual.

Robb followed me, nosing into my private life with ease. "Where did you learn to do this?"

"I thought you remembered everything?" I wouldn't bore him with a retelling, but the only real memory I had, before I became a ward of this fine state of Connecticut, was making my first paper crane when I was maybe four or five. We were in a bus station, my mother and I. We'd gone inside to keep warm and to pass the time, and she showed me how to crease those tricky paper folds. I could still see her blonde hair falling across my cold fingers as she worked. *Make a wish, Jason baby.*

I ducked into the bathroom to brush my teeth and made a point not to look in the mirror. I'm pretty sure I wouldn't like who I saw.

I wasn't a hoarder, or a drug addict. I didn't collect model trains or dress mouse skeletons in homemade clothing. But there were a lot of pieces of folded paper hanging around my home. Thousands of them. Maybe more. Robb must have noticed the paper vignettes lining every shelf, the nursery rhyme families, the pointy nativity, and the kaleidoscope *Narnia*. From his perspective, the place must look like a glorified scrap bin.

I could have fallen through the floor.

Instead, I finished brushing my teeth.

"Hey." Robb gripped my shoulder, and I flinched and dropped the toothbrush. My stitches pulled. I swear I'm not a total wimp, but I'm not a soldier either. And embarrassment hurt more than all my injuries combined. "You okay?" He frowned, and I shoved his hand away.

"No. I'm mortified. I haven't shown anyone my apartment before—except your sister—because I know I'm a little weird. I mean, obviously." I stomped back to my room.

"We're all a little weird. But this place? This isn't weird. This is art."

"This," I nodded toward a mini Jupiter floating buoyant on invisible wire, "is a hobby. Anyone with access to the Internet can make a do-it-yourself craft project. I take things to the extreme."

"No. You take things to a new level. You've built your own origami universe."

"*Exactly.*" How easily had Robb narrowed on the truth? "My own private Idaho."

What had begun as a desperate attempt to retreat from a shit reality grew into a way for me to fill an ever-deepening void. I'd moved from foster home to foster home from age six to sixteen. Most of the time, all I'd had were the clothes on my back and a paper sack from DCFS with a cheap toothbrush and a Christian coloring book. From my earliest memories, I used every scrap of paper I could find to create the things I most wanted and could never have—a pet, a friend, a family. A home.

Pathetic.

Robb's knowing eyes searched my face. "I'll never forget when you made the cranes for me. I carried them with me. And I wrote you, to say thanks, but you never responded."

"Yeah, well…some things are best left in the past." The thought of seventeen-year-old me desperately folding a thousand paper cranes for a lover who'd leave anyway, absolutely gutted me. "We were just dumb kids. It meant nothing."

"It meant something to me," Robb admitted quietly. He balanced Jupiter on a single fingertip and cast the planet into a gentle orbit. Flecks of glitter dotted the floor. "They carried me through some dark times."

I swallowed, and the sound filled the room. I couldn't go there. Not now. Not tonight. "There's a blanket and pillow in the hall closet. Couch is in the living room." *Duh.* Sleet tap-danced on the roof, and I yawned with enough emphasis my eyes watered. I skirted under a pint-sized paper moon and peeled off the itchy hospital shirt. "I need to crash."

Robb watched me undress. "You really are the vault, aren't you? Locked down so no one can get inside."

"Yup." And why did he care? I kicked off my shoes and screw the Orphan Handbook, I dropped my trousers and crawled into the cool comfort of my bed. I lay still and, as the center of my own universe, the room spun appropriately around me.

He didn't leave. "Thanks for letting me stay the night, and for letting me unload earlier."

"No problem. Thanks for taking care of me. I'm just happy to be home."

"Yeah." He lingered in the doorway, clearly at war with his thoughts again. "I can return the favor if you need me to," he said simply. He shoved his hands into his pockets. "I can be the vault, too, Jase. I'm pretty much a better listener than I am a talker, anyway. Always have been. You can still trust me."

No. I couldn't. And how could Robb ease my insipid fears and my self-imposed solitude now?

"If you want…I'm right next door."

"Sure thing. Thanks."

I sank into the pillow and squeezed my eyes shut. Footsteps creaked down the hall, and the room slowed to a halt.

CHAPTER FIVE

He slipped down the hall with a soldier's grace, on feet so light that had I not already been wide awake, shivering in my nest of blankets, waiting for the dead furnace to kick back on, I'd have missed him.

"Go away." Frosty air nipped my nose, and I burrowed deeper under the covers. My feet were blocks of ice.

"You have sharp ears." A purple shape filled the doorway.

"The better to hear you with."

"Maybe you should have enlisted instead of me." Robb stumbled over something, probably my shoes, and grumbled, "Power's out. Aren't you cold? I'm freezing."

"This happens all the time. Heat'll be back by morning."

"That's not an answer. Are you cold?"

No sense in lying. "Of course I am. There's no heat."

He hovered by the side of the bed, and a tiny light flared. Shadows played across his face, and I recognized his look.

"Shine that flashlight in my eyes one more time, and you're a dead man."

"You're six hours post-concussion, and you agreed," Mr. Calm answered. "Irritability is a sign of a worsening condition." He had to be making that crap up. The light hurt, but no more than normal, and he was quick. "Good news. Your eyes are still blue."

I blinked the spots away. Robb joking? Suspicion clouded my mind.

"Do you have a woodstove or something? A generator? A candle?" A blanket draped his shoulders, cape-like, and, ready for action, he rubbed his hands together.

"No, I have a cat—but you let him out. I usually hunker down, with the cat, and wait. I've had worse."

"Yeah? Where? I've had worse too."

"Oh, here and there. I had this foster place once, and we went all winter with no heat—"

The mattress dipped.

"What the *hell* are you doing?"

Robb perched on the bed, and my blood pressure spiked. For someone so slim, he sure took a lot of space. He made himself comfortable while I suffered palpitations.

Why was I bothered that he sat so close? Easy. I didn't trust myself alone with him. The years had flipped by, and I still wanted him.

I couldn't stop my heart from racing as he settled against the headboard. "We want to avoid hypothermia. I didn't agree to stay the night so we could both die in our sleep."

"We're not going to die." My voice cracked. "You look hearty enough. I have *stitches*. I'm not going into shock or anything." At least I hadn't been until he made himself at home on my bed. He'd yet to touch me—*not that I expected him to*—and my whole body quaked. My crotch definitely warmed in his presence.

The bed moved as he stretched full length beside me.

"Now what are you doing?"

"Relax. We're conserving heat. Is there a problem?"

"You're the problem. You're using the threat of hypothermia as an excuse to climb into my bed."

"Are you overestimating your charm, Jase?" I know he smiled. "I'm cold. The power's been off for hours, and my coat is locked in the bar. Slide over." He sounded confident, and right then, I knew I was behaving according to his plan, which was so much like the old Robb, I slid over to make room for him.

The covers lifted, and for the first time in recent memory, a man crawled inside my cocoon. His bare toe brushed my leg, and I shivered, but not from cold. No. Robb's nearness electrified me. Always had. Thank God he still had his pants on.

I didn't have pants on.

I imagined the fine hair covering his forearms and the dark fuzz on his legs, the dip of his hipbone and the deep line of his quads. He'd be muscled and lean, and at that delicious juncture where his thighs met, his skin would be delicate and pale. His familiar scent tickled my nose, and I forced myself to relax. I took a breath. "Robb. I don't want you to get the wrong idea, but you know I'm still gay, right? That hasn't changed."

"A lot of things are different about both of us, but I never thought you'd switched teams in the interim. Despite some confusion with my father's earlier message, I'm who I've always been. What's your point?"

"I'm just saying that when a man climbs into my bed, usually he's got something specific in mind, and I can't keep myself from reacting."

"You don't think hypothermia's specific?"

"Quit fucking around. I didn't hit my head that hard. What do you want? *Tell me*."

A yellow light flashed through my window as a plow struggled to clear Route Seven. The glow illuminated Robb as he turned to face me. His stare never wavered, and his steamy voice returned, the same one he'd used when we were on the stairs. "Exactly what you think I want, Jason. What I've wanted since I first saw you walk into the house tonight. *You.* Every time I've ever seen you, since the very first when you fell down the stairs and landed at my feet, I've wanted you. Always. I see you? I want to be inside you. Why is that?"

He'd intentionally flustered me earlier. He'd wanted me, but *Jesus*, I had no idea he'd lusted after me at the lake. He'd been so busy glaring and tapping his teeth together and standing apart. When Robb left the house, maybe he hadn't been running. Maybe he'd been following. He'd watched me while his mother had me in her clutches, and he hadn't stopped watching me since.

The air burned. His heart hammered across the distance. His breath mingled with mine. How easy to fall back into those arms and lose myself in the heaven of Robb Sharpe's hard body. Anything we did in my house would be free and unfettered. We could dodge history, dump accountability, and hook up like normal adult men do. No big deal. Sex didn't have to be encumbered by commitment or conversation. We could please each other and leave the heavy stuff outside the door, and *Happy Christmas to me*, we could move on. Besides, as far as I knew, he was only passing through.

I bought my lies so easily.

His chest caught when I rolled to my side and our knees touched. I found his jaw, stubbly and tight, and when I curved a palm around his hollowed cheek, he sighed and leaned into my hand. We fit perfectly.

Robb licked the center of my palm, and I sucked in frigid air. His tongue rode the edges of my blood stream, lighting a path from my hand, through my heart, and straight into my belly. With that first kiss, I hardened—seventeen again.

"You're not still freaked that I'm here?"

"Just be straight with me. If you stay, fine. If you go? Tell me. That's all I ask. I have no issues with sex, I just don't like people in my apartment. I'm sort of crazy that way."

"You're sort of crazy in every way, but I always liked crazy." His hand flattened on my lower back, and he pressed his long, lean length into me.

I brushed a kiss against his neck. His skin tasted of salt and aftershave. Then I grew bold and rubbed my palm across his shorn head the way I'd wanted to do all night. His soft hair tickled my palm. "We're just generating body heat. We're strictly by the book."

"Absolutely." Lightning quick, soldier quick actually, he covered me and pinned my wrists to the pillow. He didn't hold me like a prisoner. He held me as if he wanted me to surrender. Good thing I already had.

Fingers tightened around the bones of my wrists, and his lips teased mine until I rolled into his hips. He pushed back, huge, just like I remembered, and another tremor of lust made my ass tense.

I knew exactly where we were headed. *Exactly.*

Robb pushed to an elbow. His palm slid from my wrist, to my jaw, over my neck, down my chest, and headed straight for my crotch. "You sure?"

"Yes. Take your clothes off." I pulled at his sweater. "Why do you have so many clothes on? Take this shit off."

"You first." My boxers slid, and he dug inside the waistband until cool fingers closed around stiff flesh.

"Jesus Christ that feels good."

His tongue slipped between my lips again, his hand worked between my thighs, and I pumped into that fist. I bit his mouth, kissed his chin, sucked his neck and then I grabbed his shirt and sweater in both hands and tore his clothes over his head.

I stilled. I could count each rib with my fingertips. "What happened to you? You're so thin."

"I've gained weight, actually."

"That's impossible." I stroked the taut slab of his abs and reached low until I worked my way into his underwear. Smooth skin filled my fist, and Robb shoved my knees apart. His hard fingers bit into the flesh of my thighs. His touch thrilled me, the same way his raw words did when he whispered into my neck, *"Turn over."* His heart banged into my chest.

When I rolled to my knees, ready, his heart galloped against my back.

Fuck the cold air. Fuck the past. Fuck the future. Fuck the party. Fuck my idiotic stitches and my stupid fears. Fuck it all.

We shoved the covers to the foot of the bed and let the bedsprings scream. The headboard knocked the wall. There wasn't anyone to hear. I found everything we needed, and with his teeth on my shoulder and first his fingers and then his cock working deep inside me, I willingly let Robb Sharpe strip me from the inside.

* * * * *

I couldn't remember the last time someone stayed the night. By my best recollection? Never.

Robb tucked me into his lanky body, and the comfortable aura of spent love enveloped our warm little world. I kept sentinel until fingers of gray light reached through the frost-etched windowpanes. The night sky paled, and Robb snored gently into my hair.

His impossible blue-black hair contrasted against the stark white of his skin and the golden hair on my arms and chest. He was unbelievably pale, even compared to me, and I spent most of my time indoors tending bar. The lavender circles under his eyes were fresh and surprisingly deep.

Eventually, the furnace kicked on, and I slept.

I woke alone, sweltering under a pile of blankets, blinking at a field of dust-coated stars. Daylight, but soft. The snow had stopped. Water ran in the bathroom, so Robb hadn't bailed. Now we'd do the awkward morning-after waltz, which I preferred to do clothed, just in case things ended badly. We had a history of fucking things up, Robb and I, so I grabbed a pair of jeans from the floor, and as I slipped on a T-shirt, the bathroom door creaked, and Robb entered the hall, dressed in yesterday's party clothes and poised to run. His shirttails hung from his sweater, and his shoes were on.

"Hey." His fractured voice shot across the hall. Nothing soft or kind remained from last night, but that's not what surprised me. He was a tough customer; I didn't really expect anything less.

What rooted me in place, with my pants unzipped and my sleeve half on, was Robb himself.

Holy hell.

Morning revealed ashen skin and a locked jaw. His teeth gnashed, but he didn't flinch or shift his feet, and he wouldn't look my way either. He stared at the front door, so ready to sprint, I could almost feel his muscles tensing. Under my ridiculous paper sky, he stood like a stone, but underneath, his skin crawled with panic.

His beautiful brown eyes were red-rimmed, and worse, Robb's Adam's apple bobbed. I knew that look. I'd practically invented the "swallow your feelings" look. Robb choked those emotions down, and his gaze went from the door to the floor as he struggled for control.

Christ. I should have known the truth the second I'd seen him brooding by his parents' mantle. He'd run from the house, he'd abandoned me in the truck—he *was* different. And this difference had a name. Not a happy one.

Post-Traumatic Stress Disorder.

I thought his voice had broken, but no, something had broken Robb.

If only his silly penlight had shed light on this for me sooner, I'd have removed my head from the depths of my own ass, and I'd have asked the right question from the start. Finally, I did. "Hey. You okay, Robb? How are you?"

So little. So late.

"Fine." He watched the front door, no doubt gauging the safest escape route. Man, I'd been there a thousand times. I'd been there last night.

He finally looked my way. "I have trouble sleeping most of the time. Gets me up at night. Makes me jumpy. Parting gift from deployment they tell me. Did I wake you? I tried not to."

I shook my head. "No. Slept like a baby, actually. Thank you for that."

"How's your head?" He didn't make a single move to check my pupils, nor did he wait for an answer. "I thought I'd head back, give you some space. You seem fine today."

"I am. And I have that list from the hospital, just in case."

"Sunny'll be here soon. I called her. I hope you don't mind." His fingers drummed against his thigh and sweat glistened on his forehead.

I checked the window. "Are the roads clear? You want some coffee before you go—"

"No. Thanks. I'm good."

I trailed him to the front door, passing under a dark and dusty sky. He'd freeze if he didn't get his coat and hat from the bar. Where would he go? Back to the lake? Or was he fleeing Cornwall for good?

I stopped him with a hand on his. "Robb. Wait."

"I need to go." Robb dropped his chin and squeezed his eyes shut. "I swear it's not you."

"I know. I understand. Listen to me, Robb. *I understand.*"

"I'm sorry. I know you have some problems, with your mom leaving, and everything else, and I swore all I wanted was to see you and not complicate anything. I asked my mother to invite you. She and Sunny both. I didn't know Sunny hadn't told you."

"I figured as much. I'm glad Sunny brought me, but I did think your mom was suspiciously friendly last night."

"They're worried. That's for sure."

"They love you."

He nodded. "I can't believe...I mean last night, I didn't intend for things to go so far." He swallowed again and squeezed my fingers. "But I see you, and I can't help myself. I'm sorry. We have shitty timing."

"No regrets. You don't have to explain anything. We're old friends who reconnected at Christmas. I'm glad we did." Solid truth. Robb had given me a Christmas gift that mattered. Closure. My throat closed, but instead of damming the flood of words, I set them free. "I want only good things for you, Robb. Honestly. I wish you well."

"You deserve better. All I do is leave—but you terrified me then. And now? I want to stay, to see if this thing between us could work."

"But you can't. I understand. Sometimes, people leave. And I'm not as fragile as you think. We can pick this up some other time. I'd like that."

"You've made a great life for yourself, Jason. You should be proud." He shook my hand off, turned the knob, and Robb Sharpe disappeared from my life again.

CHAPTER SIX

"Mail's here." Donnie waltzed into the office and dumped a stack of letters onto the towering pile of bills sitting on my battered desk. Envelopes spilled into my lap, and Donnie ducked back to the bar. "Sorry, Jase!"

Just another normal, slow Wednesday in March. Donny held the front of house. I'd settled down with a cup of Earl Grey as U2 played over the bar speakers. The day was unremarkable. I had a turkey and bacon sandwich to snack on, and my laptop fired up. I found my letter opener and sorted envelopes, bills from junk, until I came across an unmarked, rain-stained letter, postmarked in California.

Weird. I sliced the envelope and, inconceivably, a crushed paper crane slid into my waiting hand. I almost dropped it as my universe tilted to a halt. Bono droned on. Glasses rattled in the bus bucket outside my office door. But I sat stupefied by a simple folded scrap of notebook paper. College ruled. The crane's striped wings were uneven, and he looked a little lame.

I glanced at the office door, who knows why? Maybe I hoped to find him standing there, because it didn't take a detective or a return address to know who'd sent me an origami bird.

I had no clue what he intended. He'd written nothing on the crane, not that he would, but I checked. At first blush, I thought maybe this crane was one of the many I'd made for him all those years ago—but no. I knew he'd folded this piece just for me. Not a single pen mark on the envelope, either. Only my name in his bold, all caps style of writing. Like he was making an important point from somewhere far across the country—JASON FERRIS, THIS BIRD'S FOR YOU.

Did a paper crane mean he'd had a change of heart? Or was he merely "thinking of you"? Was he better? Had he rested? Was he happy? Was he crazy? Why was he in California?

Did he miss me?

I dropped the little bird in the trash, crushing hope under the firm heel of experience, and moved on with my day. We'd had one night together in ten years. Yes, that one night was spectacular, but he was nuts, and I had issues.

I wrote checks and manhandled Excel. I drank tea, and the bird watched me from the wastepaper basket.

"Oh, for crying out loud." I rescued him, straightened his lopsided wings, and set him on the shelf. Paper cranes. You're not supposed to toss them. You honor their intent—you hope for the granting of a wish.

The wrinkled crane collected dust for a week, until the following Wednesday the postman delivered another small, unmarked envelope. I shut the door to my office and opened the letter with a neat slice.

He'd crafted the second crane from a plain brown paper lunch bag.

I swallowed until the lump in my throat disappeared and my eyes cleared. I cradled that little bird in my fingers. Such a tiny, simple thing.

Did Robb know? I couldn't remember telling him, but *he remembered everything.* His paper bag crane recalled all those drives with my social workers from DCFS. He'd tapped directly into the small child inside of me, forever clutching my meager belongings to my chest, braving the world alone.

I set the fragile paper bird on my office shelf to join his striped brother.

He'd be my favorite.

Another Wednesday, another plain envelope, and as the weeks turned to months, more origami birds arrived first alone, then in pairs, then groups of twenty, until a flock of fifty or a hundred cranes flew from the confines of their paper sleeves, or padded envelopes, or battered boxes, and spread their wings. They appeared in every color, newspaper print, legal pad paper, food wrappers, shopping bags, magazine pages. They came from California, Oregon, Alabama, Massachusetts, and each one looked more sure and sharp than the last.

I finally gave in and strung the cranes properly, forty rows of twenty-five each.

An army of earnest origami cranes spanned the office with a message that was impossible to ignore. They flew weightless, silently keeping me company as I worked. I couldn't miss the parallel between the desperate, youthful *come home to me* cranes I'd made at seventeen, and his careful, thoughtful *wait for me* cranes he'd made at thirty. Robb's wish filled the empty space in my office and soothed the deeper void inside my heart—where I'd always been sidelined or forgotten or ashamed.

I kept count, because I wanted to believe he'd send that perfect thousand, but the week before Thanksgiving, the cranes stopped coming.

"Knock, knock!" Sunny popped her happy face into my office on Christmas Eve. Her hair had grown over the summer, and black curls fell to her neck. She wore a loosely knit cap on her head, a long white scarf, and with tall leather boots and a black skirt and tights, she was beautiful, à la Mary Tyler Moore.

"Hey. Long time no see."

"Wow." She poked my paper bag crane with her finger. "Are they still coming?"

"Not really. Not for a few weeks." I wasn't going to revisit my disappointment, but Sunny had no problem hauling my pain right back into the open.

"Oh. Well…that's disappointing, right? I thought he'd meet his goal. He's always focused. Plus he's really good at math. How many are there?"

"I don't know. Nine hundred something." Nine hundred and eighty-seven. "Not nearly enough."

"Pfft. Right. Liar. When did you get so hardheaded? Maybe nine hundred is exactly enough. Have you thought of it that way? Maybe Robb got his wish." She plucked a yellow crane off the shelf and smiled. "Why's this one here?"

"I'm short a few. I couldn't string them. That's one of the leftovers."

"He's so cute." Sunny gently manipulated the perfectly folded wings and made him swoop across the desk. "This is a hamburger wrapper." She laughed. "Look at that. I wonder if he ate the whole burger first. I hope so. He's so skinny. But, how funny is this?"

"A lot of the cranes were like that. Newspaper stories, or comic strips. He sent a glossy of Johnny Depp dressed as a pirate. And a magazine shot of the solar system…"

Sunny kept blathering, "I wonder if he was eating his lunch and he thought—*Jason Ferris, this bird's for you.*"

"What's up, Sun? What do you need? I'm still not coming to the Christmas party."

"I'm not going yet. I wanted to see you first. Have you unfolded any of them? Maybe there's a secret message hidden inside." Sonny wiggled her eyebrows and pretended to unwrap the bird's wing.

"Don't!" I snapped the paper from her fingertips. "What the hell is wrong with you? Origami isn't about writing secret messages inside, it's about the gesture. Folding those cranes means you want something badly enough, you're willing to do something extraordinary. You don't take the asking lightly. You mean it."

"Right."

"And I told you, he stopped sending them."

"But why *did* he stop? What's he saying now, Einstein?"

"That he's busy? That he's bored? I'm sort of bored with this conversation. Don't you have some shopping to do?"

She placed the paper bird back on my office shelf. "You're such a bad liar, Jase. You're dying to know why he stopped. You want him to send the rest—how many was it?"

Sunny could be such a pest when she had a point to make, so I gave in. "Thirteen. What do you think he means?"

"I'd think he's hoping you'll be here when he comes back. That was your wish, right?"

CHAPTER SEVEN

Sunny's Mini Cooper made a left at Cornwall's one and only traffic light, and I lurked like a creep behind a framework of tiny twinkling lights. She'd missed the party. Her mother would have a cow, but I was glad she'd stayed.

I waited until her taillights vanished into the squall. The light swung above the empty intersection. Snow hid her tire tracks and soon, there was no sign of her having passed through town.

She'd given me a Christmas present and for the first time, I'd forgotten to get her something in return. I should just write the Orphan Handbook and then dedicate it to her. She'd like that.

I flipped the bar sign to *Closed* and began the unpleasant task of wiping empty tables with a soaked rag. The candles were snuffed and stored, the stock reshelved, and Christmas music warbled from the bar speakers. I should've changed the CD, but that required a trip to the office and, call me crazy, I'd grown tired of my office lately.

I swiped the tabletop, and the overhead lights blinked a warning a millisecond before the room plunged into absolute black.

"*Son of a bitch.* Not again."

Minutes flipped by. The scent of old booze and fresh vinegar lingered in the air. Tick. Tock. Total fucking darkness. Soft shadows poured in from the front windows, but the lights stayed defiantly off, including our emergency light. I guess I should have changed the bulb.

I headed to the bar to retrieve a flashlight, feeling my way through the settling gloom with outreached hands and careful footsteps. Through the window, the snowy world remained dark. The sidewalks were empty. Not a single light shone in our postage stamp-sized town. One in the morning and the quiet town slept. Cold crept under doors and between the cracks, and soon, pipes would freeze in time for the holiday.

We'd have the lights back by morning. We always did.

I'd almost made my way to the end of the bar when the front door blasted wide and a frigid breeze blew a shadow into the vestibule. I nearly crapped myself with fear.

I stopped dead, cursed silently, and pulled myself together as the door slammed. A shape dissolved into the murky corner.

Maybe Santa Claus had come to deliver my heart's desire, but I didn't believe in Santa anymore.

A pair of heavy boots stomped on the rubberized entry rug. "Anyone home?"

I found my voice. "We're closed."

"Oh. Well, the door was unlocked, and the light was on when I came up the hill. I figured you were still open."

"Well, I'm not. The bar closes at one. It's after one." Not to mention it was Christmas Eve. Normal people were in bed, dreaming of sugarplum fairies or credit card bills or whatever normal people dreamed of, before getting ready for the big day ahead. I sighed. "Can I help you? I can't do much with the power out."

"Yeah. Actually, I'm looking for a ride."

I looked toward the window. "A ride?"

"Home," he clarified. "For Christmas. I'm trying to get home for the holiday."

"Uh. Maybe you should call someone? Like a family member."

"It's supposed to be a surprise." Green light flared—a cell phone—and my heart skipped so hard I took a full step back.

What the hell was wrong with me? I needed to chill. Sunny had filled my mind with all that crap about hopes and dreams, but this guy was just some poor slob trying to catch a ride home.

By the phone's glow, a bearded jaw appeared. Curls swept over a broad brow line. A pair of serious eyes absorbed the green light like a predator as he waved the phone. "No service."

No way. Sunny couldn't be right.

The light disappeared, and the room blackened. "Can I come in?"

Right. Where were my manners? I should let the guy in. Come in, sit down, warm up. Can I get you something? *Where the fuck have you been? Where are my stupid birds?*

But he wasn't Robb, Mr. Ready For Action. This guy just waited meekly in the doorway.

I found my voice. "Sure. Landline's down. It's usually the first thing to go. Is your car stuck? Do you need a push?"

"No. My ride didn't show. I had to walk from the bus station."

"Bus station? What bus station?" There wasn't a bus stop for ten miles at least.

"New Milford." His boot scraped.

"You walked? *Here?* The whole way? That's a hike." He must be half frozen and soaked to the skin.

"I had someplace I wanted to be." His outline approached, a purple shape against the darkened window. A chair wobbled when he bumped the back. "Ow. Shit."

The closer he came, the more my skin prickled, until he hovered unthreateningly near the bar. He leaned against the railing, like Riley's was open for business and he wanted to order a round.

I stalled. "Can I get you a drink? Something warm? I have some coffee leftover."

"Sure. I'm freezing."

Honestly, if I weren't scared and alone and tired and suspicious as hell, and if this night wasn't Jesus's birthday, I'd be irritated. The bar was closed. It was Christmas. Officially. And Robb Sharpe was a million miles away, folding cranes from Christmas cards, or soaking sun in Mexico, or sleeping happily beside some other man. "Are you... where did you say you were from?"

"I didn't," he whispered. Definitely not Robb. His voice would have ricocheted across the bar like gunfire.

I slid behind the countertop and searched fruitlessly for a flashlight. Not finding one, I gave up and managed to pour lukewarm coffee into what might be a clean mug. Who could tell? My eyes adjusted to the interior of the room. I should still light a few candles. Chase away the ghosts. The bartender in me had to ask, "You want a shot?"

"No thanks. Don't drink."

Backlit by the blue of the window, he moved on soldier's feet, and when he rounded the end of the bar, his pace increased.

"What are you doing?" I retreated until my ass hit the sink.

"What do you think I'm doing?"

He was on me in a blur. I couldn't run, or leap over the counter. I couldn't overpower him or dodge past him. Not because he had inches and pounds and muscle on me. No. I couldn't run because, damn, I didn't want to.

Cold air clung to his coat, and ice seeped into my skin. He found my wrist and pressed me to the back wall. Hot breath scorched my ear, and even before he said a word, my body knew him.

Robb.

"Jesus Christ, Jason, don't you even know me? This is the second fucking time you didn't recognize me."

"The lights are out!"

"I came halfway around the fucking planet, carried your Christmas present ten miles through a goddamn blizzard in the middle of the night, and you offer me piss-warm coffee and try to knock me out? It hasn't been that long."

"It's been long enough."

He laughed, and his beard scraped my neck. Hair brushed my cheek. His voice—he had a voice and not that crow-like caw from last year—broke me.

My heart hiccupped against his chest and relief made my knees rubbery. "Goddamn you. You could have called."

"And ruin the surprise? I didn't know my ride wouldn't show, and the phones don't work. My parents are having their party. I didn't want them to know I was back yet. I wanted to see you first. I wanted time alone."

Robb held me by the wrist and by the chin—by the nuts if you want the whole truth—and I still couldn't believe he'd come home. "Where did you come from?"

Snow sizzled against the window. "School."

"What?"

"Med school. I told you I wasn't a doctor yet. I planned to rectify that. I started in September. I've been a little busy."

"And…how are you?"

"I'm good. Almost great. And I want to start fresh, Jason." My shirt was soaked, but I held tight. "I'm here, and I'm asking you if you want to try again."

"I didn't think you'd come back."

"I know." He twisted to reach into his coat and placed a small package in my hand. "Did you get my message?"

"Which one?" *I'm thinking of you. I miss you. I'm coming back for you.* "There were so many. Nine hundred and eight seven."

"Now there's a thousand."

His lips were warm. His frozen jacket fell from his shoulders, and I dug my fingers into the glory of his newly grown hair. *He had hair.* He smelled of winter, of trees, of night, of peace and security, of snow and stardust. He was the light filling my darkness, and he radiated the thing I desired most in the entire world—the warm comfort of home.

I opened my heart, and, finally, I let Robb Sharpe all the way inside. Exactly where he belonged.

ABOUT THE AUTHOR

When not working from her home in the rolling hills of north-western Connecticut, best-selling author L.B. Gregg can be spotted in coffee shops from Berlin to Singapore to Panama—sipping lattes and writing sweet, hot, often funny stories about men who love men.

For more info, visit L.B.'s website at http://lbgregg.com.

TITLES BY L.B. GREGG

**THE MEN OF SMITHFIELD SERIES
(ALSO AVAILABLE IN AUDIO)**

Mark and Tony

Seth and David

Max and Finn

Adam and Holden

Sam and Aaron

THE ROMANO AND ALBRIGHT SERIES

Catch Me If You Can

Trust Me If You Dare

With This Bling

THE CORNWALL NOVELLAS

Dudleytown

Simple Gifts (also available in audio)

**OTHER NOVELLAS
(ALSO AVAILABLE IN AUDIO)**

Mistletoe at Midnight

How I Met Your Father

There's Something About Ari

Waiting for Winter